MW01277104

Returning to Center

(A Collection of Stories, Vignettes and Thoughts)

by Billy Ironcrane

This is a work of fiction. Characters, events, places, and incidents are either the product of the author's imagination or are used fictitiously. Everything portrayed has been drawn from the author's imagination and is not to be construed as real. Any semblance to actual persons, living or dead, events, or locales is entirely coincidental.

Copyright ©2018 Bill Mc Cabe

All rights reserved. No part of this publication may be reproduced, distributed, or transmitted in any form or by any means, including photocopying, recording, or other electronic or mechanical methods, without the prior written permission of the author, except in the case of brief quotations embodied in critical reviews, and certain other noncommercial uses permitted by copyright law.

For permissions contact:

www.ironcrane.com/html/contactus.html

Published by:
Mc Cabe and Associates
Tacoma, WA.

Cover Design Mc Cabe and Associates
Cover image by Bobbi Youtcheff "My Favorite Restaurant"
Author Photo by Doug Goodman

ISBN: 978-1-7324154-1-6
Library of Congress Control Number: 2018950900

*To my wife Thongbai, a bold and
courageous partner in the unending pursuit.
And to Jennifer. Undaunted by limitations, facing
all uncertainty with the heart of a lion.*

Contents

Part 1 Emergence

Part 2 Evolution

Part 3 Actualizaiton

Epilogue

Early iterations of these pieces first appeared in the following publication:

"The Man From Southern Mountain" first published in TaeKwonDo Times (July 1988),
Editor Carol Davis Hart, Copyright 1988 by Bill Mc Cabe.

"The Water Principle" first published in TaeKwon Do Times (March 1989) as "The Martial Arts Water Principle," Editor Carol Davis Hart, Copyright 1989 by Bill Mc Cabe.

"Three Times Around the Circle" first published in TaeKwonDo Times (January 1990), Editor Carol Davis Hart, Copyright 1990 by Bill Mc Cabe.

Returning
To
Center

Introduction

Allow me to extend my hand in friendship.

That's how Billy and I first met. When you've spent a lifetime trying to find answers to questions which swirl endlessly about, it gets lonely. That seems to have become my life's purpose, always asking the hard questions, then clinging on to the answers like a pit bull fighting for his life. It's not easy you see. I believe there can be truth, and I believe you can count on it to dial in your very existence. Center. Trust me on this my new friend, that's where you want to be. Right smack in the middle of this wonderful creation. How you think, how you move. Smooth and fluid, even against the stiffest resistance. Even when little pieces of you break off, and you feel like you're falling apart.

We met in Spires. the Alder tavern. He just seemed to be there, wedged in a dark corner, watching and studying everything. I could see he was searching for answers too, a kindred spirit perhaps. I didn't say anything at first, just walked up to him hoping to feel what he was about. Why not? Just about everyone else in the joint had it in for me. In fact, no one else seemed to notice, or pay any attention to him. Maybe I approached him to see if he was for real, or some shadow from my wine soaked imagination.

He stood to my approach, and looked toward me with compassion and understanding. He seemed to know me, and with his eyes, acknowledged my never ending struggle. Who knew it could be so obvious? This wasn't something I did often in those days, but I smiled and reached my hand forward in camaraderie. It's been that way between us ever since.

It's only natural he would invite me to do this introduction. How could I resist? He knew that of course. He did however warn me not to ramble, so I won't take much more of your time. What follows will tell you what you need to hear, and to take with you going in.

First. These stories recount the common search for a center within. A place of respite from turmoil and uncertainty. A place from where we can make sense and come to terms with all which confronts us. You'll come upon at least one mystic, and many varieties of masters. You'll find some hidden away, and some right there in front of your nose. They might be soldiers, business men, martial artists, drop outs or saviors, or just overwrought people trying to cope with reality while reaching for awareness and peace. You'll see how they change, and what changes them, and though not easily expressed in words, you may come to understand why, and how they have such profound impact on who and whatsoever they encounter.

Finally, you should know this. I mention it with humility and would almost prefer not to. But Billy insisted, and his instincts rarely miss the mark. Much of what follows is about me, at times directly, most times indirectly. Know that going in. It might help to think of me as the common thread at the center. There ... I believe I've said enough.

Take care my friend. Be well, and do well. Enjoy what follows and remember me downstream.

Mason McKenzie

Part 1- Emergence

Meeting Master

Frequently, would-be seekers puzzle over how to find a genuine "master." Like any good shopper, they want the best from the outset. Unfortunately, many wrong turns and detours will divert their paths before they find what they think they are looking for (if they ever do). Genuine masters may not be what they really want, but they don't know that in the beginning and you can't tell them so they'll understand. Masters don't go around with neon halos floating over their heads. If anything, they are like trees, very powerful, very balanced, and appearing so ordinary you wouldn't otherwise notice them. Sometimes rife with foibles, few are looking to recruit disciples, preferring to keep their focus on life, and mastering its complex processes and responsibilities. Their teachings embody love, compassion and in a back hand way, generosity. They don't tolerate fools, arrogance, or selfishness, preferring to avoid them entirely. They can be remote, even aloof. They make worthwhile friends, but will never be your proxy father, mother, brother or sister (even though you might choose to think they are). They are never Santa Claus! They will be your teacher, nothing more, nothing less. Where they're at relative to you, committing to be your teacher represents a huge commitment. If you ever get confused about the relationship, they will feel you are wasting their time and deal with it summarily. Lastly, when you have finally learned well enough to pass knowledge on to others, don't expect your master to graciously accept your doing so on his or her turf or behalf. More likely, you will be encouraged by cold shoulder to forge a path of your own. It may even feel as though you've been kicked out. Why does that gift of ultimate freedom seem so harsh to so many??? What follows is a composite of several experiences . I offer it as an aid in your search.

He gripped the stick in his hand...reminiscing. After a momentary silence, he passed it to me.

I knew it well, for in our group, it recorded our individual apprenticeships, the years of toil, discipline, challenge and growth. It was the gauge by which he charted our development. Etched onto its skin was his special shorthand, commemorating our progress with his peculiar array of scribbles, pictographs, slashes and notches. Some of his shorthand was nothing more than blemishes resulting from impacts against our bodies, which sometimes presented as targets to his admonishments. It fit the hand nicely, and once I even saw it stop the death cut of an attacker's sword. It weighed light, but projected strength. It made a fine weapon.

In training, I learned to use the stick, and a multitude of other objects as weapons. I should clarify. I learned to become one with my surroundings, and to translate objects from my environment into purpose.

But the significance of this particular stick went beyond that.

When we met, I was already established as a martial artist. Nearly half my life had been spent mastering the tricks of fighting, and I had more than "paid my dues." I held the rank of Black Belt in several respected systems.

Our first encounter was at a children's Karate tournament in San Francisco. Now that I think of it, wherever he went, people seemed to gravitate toward him. If he walked into a room, the floor would seemingly tilt his way, and before long, people, as though standing on phantom bearings, would glide toward where he stood. That first time, I felt I was the only one on the scene not aware of who he was. Everyone else seemed to be contending for his attention.

It would be fair to say he could be flamboyant. He was already sixty-five years old, but did not look a day beyond forty. His hair remained black, and grew in flowing curls, attesting to his heritage. The well-trimmed beard and mustache highlighted his time wizened visage.

There was always an air of cologne, and the ever present glasses. He was short in stature, his body habitus being perhaps as short as one could possibly be without taking on a disproportional appearance. At the same time, his weight ranged as high as one hundred and ninety pounds, though, because of his lifetime of training, he seldom ever looked to weigh more than one hundred and forty. Of course, this produced many startled expressions when he challenged strangers to lift him, then remained glued to the ground.

When you expect to be lifting one hundred and forty pounds, one hundred and ninety becomes like a ton. He would call it a "trick of the mind." Indeed, a trick of the mind manifesting as fact.

On that first day, he demonstrated his art to the children, their parents, and other instructors. He wore a black silk uniform in the Chinese style. It presented a rich and extravagant appearance in its sheen and rustle as he moved. Around his waist, he wore a red sash, signifying he was a master.

He performed a breaking demonstration. Of course, he did the usual tricks with bricks and boards, but it wasn't long into the demonstration that I knew this gentleman was special. To the awe of the crowd and myself, his assistants brought in a bucket of rocks. These were of the type common to river beds. The rocks were passed to the crowd for scrutiny. There was no trick or gimmick to this man's art. A rock found its way into my hands and I studied the smooth rounded surface which had been sculpted by the passage of time and water. It had the appearance of a flattened football, perhaps as long, but half as wide at its thickest part. As an experienced martial artist, I knew that breaking such an object would be a bone crunching challenge. I thought, "This can't be done."

He looked toward me and asked that I bring it to him. I assured all present the stone had passed my inspection.

Approaching, I studied him closely. Stunts like this were responsible for the countless broken wrists and hands of lesser martial artists. He, however, was quite nonchalant about the whole procedure, and if anything, appeared to be having a genuinely good time despite the obvious skepticism among the spectators.

I stood back, and lowered so my eyes were level with the stone, its ends now sitting on vertical steel columns. Silence enveloped the hall as he readied himself for the blow.

He directed his attention to the stone. Of all, I stood closest. I could see as he laid his left hand carefully on the surface to steady its position. His eyes, face, and demeanor took on a look far removed from the crowd of children, parents, curiosity seekers, and would be critics scrutinizing his effort. I wondered what story lay beneath his gaze. In an instant, he raised high his right arm and sent his knife hand crashing to the rock, pulverizing into fragments what was indestructible only seconds before.

He did the same, again and again, rock after rock, until not one of all present, could doubt this gentleman and his singular talents.

Later in the day, we had a chance encounter, and I complimented his extraordinary breaking demonstration. He extended his hand in a warm courteous fashion, and as we shook I noted the supranormal size and hardness of his right hand. I was to learn later that in addition to his knowledge of many styles, he was a proponent of the "iron hand."

Being a Black Belt I was invited and took part in judging and refereeing the events which followed. As the afternoon progressed, he and I had opportunity to judge together in some of the competition rings. I didn't know it, but I had become the target of his scrutiny, even when he, as he often did, ran off to play with the kids, or to wrestle with one of his many friends, sometimes rolling around on the floor like a playful cub. Other instructors were put off by these lapses of formality. I was bemused.

I once heard a famous martial artist comment, "Every master is an unexpected surprise waiting to happen." If this be true, there could be no doubt Sensei[1] fell into the mold. He was always "about to happen." At times, after we became close, his playing would make him seem almost childlike. There were occasions when I was the center referee of a ring and he was one of my associate judges. He would walk off, and I would physically have to retrieve him, and return him to his designated station so we could continue the matches. As I was to learn, within this same person was the mind of a martial arts genius, a consummate disciplinarian, and a master whose concentration, intention, indomitable spirit, and indomitable will were such that what was impossible for many, became ordinary for him. However, it was during the course of our playful exchanges, and "fooling around" that the seeds of familiarity were planted between us, and in time, he came to call me "friend."

Eventually, he tendered invitation to visit his home school and secluded work out area. I later learned that tolerating his playfulness was my first test, which, had I not passed, would have relegated me to the eternal company of those whom he reckoned to be lesser martial artists.

---

[1] Japanese word for "teacher." Literally, "one born before."

As often happens when meeting new people, one tends not to follow up on an invitation. It was so with me. In fact, he invited several times over again, and each time I assured I would come, but did not. Was it possible I sensed my many years of training were at risk? Would I find I could not measure well against his art? Frankly, I didn't know if I could deal with having invested years in martial disciplines, only to find my skills wanting as this man blasted through all that I had come to rely upon.

Nearly two years passed from the time of first invitation until I came to visit his school. Such are human foibles! I was literally transported to the site by an intervening common friend sent by him to commandeer my presence.

This is what took place the first fateful day...

When I arrived, his class was in session. It was a "camp" in the woods, containing a staggering array of machines, devices, training aids and tools which constituted the essence of what he hoped to transmit to his students through his art. Imagine yourself falling into a Kung Fu movie, the beginning part, where they're training in the temple. That's how I felt. I realized there was no room for my ego with these students and humbly asked if I could join as they went through their workout. He radiated an expression of sheer delight at my request and motioned with an ebullient "Sure!" for me to join the in-progress session. I did, and before long, became part of another demonstration of this man's skills. His students started working with weapons. One with a knife; another with a staff; still another with a sword; and so on as far as I could see. Extending his welcome, he allowed I should take a weapon and work some attacks against him.

Incredible as it may seem, we spent hours of me attacking with various weapons, and he disintegrating my attacks instantly.

In a sense, it began to feel as though Sensei were reading my mind, or perhaps was even commanding me to come with certain attacks which he had already prepared responses for. The uneasy feeling in my gut conjured images of standing on the edge of a cliff, staring into emptiness.

As the formalities relaxed, we went through dozens, maybe hundreds more attacks and responses in rapid succession. Nothing I did could penetrate his defense, unless he allowed. Conversely, nothing I did could prevent him from penetrating my own defense. At times, he took on the demeanor of stone, and became an immovable object. Suddenly, he was a puff of air, instantly disappearing from my view, then reappearing over my head after I had been delivered to the ground and done in. The knowledge I carried within me was meaningless! I was discovering levels of personal humility I never knew would be demanded of me! Who was I to argue with harsh fact?

By day's end, I had to look within myself and make a choice.

As we were about to part, he called me his "special friend" and assured I would be welcome to work with him "anytime," and that he would "show me anything" I wanted to know.

As I weighed his offer, I knew I was free to leave and pretend I had not experienced his art, free to continue wearing my Black Belts with the dignity accorded them by peers in the martial arts community. But if I were to acknowledge this gentleman as my teacher, I would have to go beyond my past training, which on that day seemed of little significance.

I chose the latter course, and the gentleman who was already my friend, became my teacher.

To commemorate the event, he pulled out a piece of roughly hewn rattan, cutting off a segment which later, I measured at twenty-eight inches in length. He said from that day, the stick and I would be as one, and just as he would shape, and carve the stick, so would I be shaped and remade by the things I was about to do, to learn, and to experience. He added when my time with him had run its course, the stick would be full. He would deliver the finished totem into my hands, to commemorate our friendship and the path I had decided to take. He continued, "Colors as you know them can turn you into a blinded fool. The sounds you recognize make you deaf to the natural symphony. You will learn to empty your heart of the token passions that drive men to wildness. You will learn to truly see and to hear. In like fashion, the flavors and tastes that you chase can numb the tongue. I will teach you restraint. Out there, you live in a cyclone, which ultimately cannot fail but to cloud your heart and steal your ability to think clearly and decisively. I will teach you discipline. The mindless pursuit of rank and prestige is a path that leads to no destination. They may come to you of their own accord if you are worthy, but then again they may not. To be worthy is enough. Let that guide your efforts. There is no rank here, just student and teacher, and what passes between the two. When you are finished here, you will be empty, and awake, and you will have the stick as my testament, as well as your sash. From today, be guided by what you feel, and not by what you think you feel. Forsake causes and effects, and become the process."

Thus began my journey...

The Man from Southern Mountain

In his youth, he had been a scholar. His knowledge, wit, and counsel brought him fame throughout the land. Before reaching age twenty, he had become first counselor in the court of the Western Emperor. His influence was great. All feared his disfavor.

But power and influence did not suit him well. The land was torn with conflict, as it had been for as long as anyone could remember. Of the people in the empire, there were four classes. First, the farmers, upon whom all depended for the essentials of life. Then came the soldiers and their leaders, who eternally struggled to make real the visions and dreams of the Emperor. Next were the intellectuals, survivors of countless batteries of tests, interviews, and progressively difficult assignments, upon whose judgment the policies of state hinged. Lastly, the aristocracy, topped by the Emperor, the "divine" center around whom swirled all affairs of the kingdom, as the currents of time rippled onward.

His stature as first counselor brought him no joy. There was no end to it all, no outcome, no resolution. He longed for the day he could be finished with it, and assured of the Emperor's "Well done, counselor!" Others had preceded him. Countless others would follow. But the cycle of birth, suffering, and death continued unabated. Was this what brought Siddhartha Gautama to near despair before his final awakening? Was this what the Buddha came to resolve under the Bo tree?

Taking the Emperor's leave, he left the court to enter the temple. He knew his request could not be refused, even the Emperor must defer to the gods, albeit in his case with no small degree of protest. Temple life proved austere, and its simplicity was a marked change from the always available pleasures of the courtly environment. He studied the Tao, and the life of the Buddha. He spent days in deep meditation, looking for the stillness within, which his seniors promised would free him from all distractions and doubts concerning the very purpose of his existence.

In time, it became clear the way of the temple was not for him. The meditations and rigors of temple life actually distracted him from the inner peace he sought, as had the pleasures and gratifications of the court.

With the Abbot's permission, he returned to the world. The Abbott gave his blessing, explaining that "Each must define his own course, and in the Tao, all courses have equal merit."

He journeyed far to the south, and saw first hand rampant disease, hunger, and all the rages of war. One day, while viewing a headless corpse left unburied on a remote and forgotten battlefield, he experienced what the Abbot might have described as "an enlightenment." Enveloped by the stench, eyeing the vermin veering from his gaze within the armor shell, he saw with absolute clarity how his well reasoned counsel to the Emperor had set into action the string of events leading directly to this body laying at his feet at this spot at this precise moment in time.

"Was he ever a real person? Couldn't this simply be a 'lesson' from the Tao? Yes, I must be dreaming." In the stream of sunlight, he saw his face in the armor. "It all makes so much sense now. This man, his fate, and I are all one and the same."

As though awakening from a dream, he bent forward to touch the swollen corpse. But the harsh edge of stench cut deeply into his senses and snapped him instantly back to reality.

"This is not a dream!"

Thinking back to his days at court, he wondered, "Why couldn't I see this possibility when I was the Emperor's counselor? What good was my learning, my years of training, my dedication to the absolute if this be the outcome?"

Having buried the body, he continued his journey. After a period of aimless wandering, he arrived at the Southern Mountains. There he left the world once again.

For once, he was truly alone. Here was a whole new experience, a whole new knowledge. Even in the temple, in the deep silence, there was always the awareness of others nearby. Silence, but never solitude. Here, the solitude was genuine, supreme, and like the surrounding air, a living part of his environment.

He learned first the lessons of hunger. He was far too removed from his ancestral past to rely on natural instincts to find his food. For the first three days, he was helpless and ate nothing.

It was an eternity. Never had he thought of nothing but food for so long, with such degree of intensity. For every waking minute of every waking hour, he focused on his hunger. And the hunger grew, and as the hunger grew, he focused all the more strongly on it, until time itself seemed to stand still. Tortuous hours became days, and days months. It was the fourth day when he found food, but by then he had experienced eternity!

In his early forages, he focused on the accessible. There were the frogs, the snakes, the cattails, the swamp roots, and the berries. But none of it came easy. Even the food of the temple seemed extravagant in comparison. He fasted often.

The first month, he derived his nourishment from the crystal waters, and the warm radiant rays of the sun. To supplement his meager fare, he ate the leftovers of travelers and highwaymen. Without at first realizing the change, he began to follow the natural cycles. When tired, he rested; when hungry, he foraged for food. All very simple, but bringing to him a deep sense of harmony within his new environment.

He came to know the plants and the ways of the animals. Meat and sustenance soon grew to abundance. What once took a whole day to garnish, could now be done quickly. After the first pangs of hunger, he would begin his search for food, and before long, his stomach was full.

There were others like him. Like him that is, in that for reasons of their own, they choose to live in the Southern Mountains. There were the outlaws, the deserters, the mystics, the brigands, and the outcasts. Initially, he watched them from afar, and wondered what had brought them into the wilderness. Sometimes, his curiosity would be overwhelming, and he would maneuver to vantage points closer to their camps. He came to be so skilled at this, that he could come within hearing range of their voices, and not be discovered. That was how he kept current on the affairs of men.

One morning, he awoke and inexplicably, he could "see." To "see" went far beyond the normal capacity of sight. For example, on that first morning, he "saw" a band of soldiers entering the valley across the saddle of the white pony. That mountainous ridge was one full day's walk away, but he "saw" with certainty, and with unshakable confidence. On other occasions, he "heard," he "smelled," and he "felt." It was as though he had become one with all things. When a bird flew overhead, he could "become" the bird, willing his consciousness into the creature, and instantly see down upon his physical body from dizzying heights.

The very next evening he visited the soldiers' camp, sat in their midst as they talked, partook of their food, and shared the warmth of their campfire. The soldiers however, never knew he had been there.

As legends and stories often arise to explain the unknown, there came to be the legend of the man from Southern Mountain. In the night, when travelers heard strange sounds, or saw strange shapes flitter about in the darkness, or when they would awake to find food missing from their sacks, they would always exclaim, "Looks like we had a visit from the man of the mountain!" That was how it was.

To survive on the mountain, he became one with the animals. Even at first, when he still ate the flesh of animals to survive, he would walk undetected up to his prey, and silently issue the coup de grace, as though he and the prey were fait accompli, sharing in some unwritten script.

With infinite patience, he would study the animals closely, all the animals, from the bears, to the panthers, to the lowliest insects.

He had learned lessons that no book could tell, no intellect could pass on. He learned that the human entity was a composite of thought, substance, emotion, and experience. Experience was the driver for all growth, and it was man's tie to the worldly environment, as natural a tie as the stem holding a leaf to the tree. The path to knowledge and understanding was not to be found in books, in the halls of power, or in shaping the destinies of men. The mountain had taught him otherwise. There were other truths to be gathered.

No one knows what became of the man from Southern Mountain. Legends abound. Some say he left the mountains to rally the villages in campaigns against marauding warlords. Others say he founded a temple to his liking, where he consecrated his newfound knowledge to the Buddha. There are even reports that he became one of the immortals and to this day is said to visit the camps of those entering the mountain's sanctuary.

What is certain is that eventually, the Emperor sent his agents to retrieve the errant counselor and return him to court. At first, a polite refusal was sufficient for the agents to leave without event. Of course, before long, the Emperor lost patience. The refusals offended his personal sense of dignity. Frustrated, he sent his secret police to capture the hermit.

Then the confrontations began.

Reports filtered back to the Emperor of a man who fought with supernatural fury and who, on one occasion, had singlehandedly disarmed and disabled fifteen officers of the imperial guard. Such a feat was unheard of in the land, and only caused the Emperor's concerns to heighten.

What the imperial guard did not know was that during his years in the wilderness, the man from Southern Mountain had become whole, melding the lessons of the mountain into an alphabet of motion, making him invincible to those of lesser discipline.

From the bear, he learned strength and power, and commitment in attack. Instantly, he could issue forth with unnerving sounds while swipes of his "paws" easily smashed the strongest suits of armor.

Or he could become the panther, systematically slashing out and weakening his opponent before going in for the kill.

Even as the lowly grasshopper, he could be there, but not there, whenever and wherever you attacked. The animal variations were endless. He and they were one. For one opponent, he was the eagle, for another, the monkey, and for still another, the mantis.

However, the source of all worldly power, even that of the mountain, was the dragon. Dragon rules positive karma, and from his throne, protects the nourishing forces of creation. He governs survival. He rules the natural order. The hermit came to understand dragon as the common denominator between himself, the animals, the mountain, and his maker. The dragon is master of position. Though words are weak in description, an intellectual might say that, "The dragon is always where his power is greatest, and his power is greatest wherever he may be." But the hermit recognized that dragon's strength was rooted intimately in its relationship to the environment. When the dragon sets, there are never openings. When you move against the dragon, you leave yourself open. There are no other possibilities.

The man of Southern Mountain had learned about the dragon as an attitude. He was always in dragon posture, whether walking through the woods, relieving himself, or sleeping. There simply were no openings. Though the Emperor's men could not comprehend this unknown force, they recognized their helplessness and, without exception, returned in disgrace to the court. Unable to risk further embarrassment, the Emperor eventually tired of the pursuits, and returned to his wars, relying upon alternate counsel. The warlords too, found they were better served continuing their greedy quests elsewhere and leaving this man to his mountain.

When the mountain was finally safe from marauders, and soldiers, and brigands, many others came, hoping to learn from the "powerful holy man." Of the many who wandered directionless through the woods of Southern Mountain, a handful were chosen to be students. As for the others, the man from Southern Mountain was not to be found, and probably did not even exist.

Of the chosen, all in time returned to the world of men. it was the wish of the teacher that once they learned the lessons of Southern Mountain, they should return to the affairs of men and serve as guides for others.

These students taught others, and they in turn taught more still. My own master once said that more than forty generations had passed from when the hermit first revealed his knowledge to another. If pressed, he could name the entire line of teachers, from the man on Southern Mountain, to his own master, head Abbot of Fragrant Woods Monastery in the highlands between China and Korea.

Unlike the other arts which varied from teacher to teacher, the style of the animals lingered as a philosophy of images. Like the dragon, the animal styles were forms or thoughts, which adapted to suit the individual idiosyncrasies of each person. The forms themselves remained pure and unchangeable, like beacons in a world darkened by ignorance.

And for that reason, whenever there was a question to be resolved, one only had to reach into the images within to find his own Southern Mountain and once again ... speak to the master.

Waiting in Line

When McKenzie served in the military, he trained at special schools. This included language, electronics, interrogation, information processing, pretty much whatever you can think of that served the covert netherworld. Though serving in uniform, he trained with students of all ranks from all services, as well as from various government agencies. He often dressed as a civilian. It was an interesting mix, and constantly challenged his perceptions.

One such episode arose when he became aware of shortages at the dining hall.

Typically, meal time would be of limited duration. Schedules were tight. Cafeteria lines would be long. It was never fun nor convenient to get stuck at the end of the line. Long standing protocol allowed commissioned officers and government agency staff direct access to the front of the line. This chafed McKenzie. It rubbed hard against his blue collar sense of social decorum.

Nevertheless, as a practical person, McKenzie would race from class to dining hall making sure to arrive early as possible, assuring he would be close to the front. Not infrequently, after securing a position and nearing entry, he found himself slipping further back as the stream of officers and agency staff arrived and stepped ahead.

McKenzie, a patient and centered person, could normally see past this nonsense, except that somewhere, in some thinly buried space he kept for scores, he collected the names and faces of those who perpetuated this practice. Long experience taught him things like this evened out over time, and to that possibility he always kept a ledger.

But here's what really got to him!

Mindful of these proclivities, it didn't take long for McKenzie to notice other patterns emerging. Often, after the ranking group entered to dine, McKenzie followed in only to find the meal offerings wanting. Read that to mean the meat and deserts were gone, as were the milk and coffee, and what was left for guys like him were some potatoes, maybe lettuce, string beans if lucky, all to be washed down with some lightly flavored water. He began to lose weight.

The first couple weeks, he accepted it was because the cafeteria was so poorly managed. It wouldn't have been the first time he encountered it. He assumed initially that everyone was getting the same fare. He was younger then, and much less prone to reading nefarious intent into what, in his later years, would have been obvious. That is until one day, one of the officers from language class wanted to chat regarding some lessons. To facilitate, he brought McKenzie with him to the line's head. Talking with the officer, McKenzie noticed on entering there was a full serving of multiple selections of meat, side dishes, deserts, juice, milk, you name it.

Perhaps it emanated from his keenly developed sense of propriety, or perhaps it was the deep rooted inner city reservoir of rage. It simmered like a dragon in the well begging for an excuse to emerge. His officer companion noticed only a momentary turn of McKenzie's head, and their dialogue continued uninterrupted, but in that brief instant McKenzie had scanned and registered every face in the food line and the serving area behind, settling on the noncom in charge, and three of his cronies, who were very busy, but not serving, just looking out. McKenzie had of course experienced those cautionary stares before. Life in the city meant always being on the lookout. For opportunities, and for threats.

To counter the weight drop, from the beginning, he made it his routine to head into town every other night to eat some real meals at his own expense. He didn't have much cash to spare, but there were no alternatives. He could deal with the expense, but now he knew the "privileged" group was getting everything he wasn't. Those less favored were getting whatever was left, literally, the crumbs, plus some. Shafted again!

He tried to raise his concerns within the command structure, to no avail. He wasn't a rat, he was looking only to move on, not to take anyone down (unless there were no other options). He told the up channel that food was running out before meal hour was half done, large numbers of personnel (He didn't say "enlisted personnel." That wouldn't have gained traction) were not getting their full meals.

No one believed what he was saying. Typical responses would be, "We're eating in the same mess hall as you, and we don't see anything wrong."

Of course, from their spots in line, all creation looked different! Is it not wondrous how perspective can blind for some, while granting hard insight to others!

There was a Marine Captain in his class. He was a professional soldier, with a chestful of ribbons from prior campaigns. The officer had early on taken notice of McKenzie, recognizing the emerging potential. More likely, he was interested in what he had seen of McKenzie's training regimen at the gym, which included a healthy serving of the combat arts. Sometimes they sparred. He liked that McKenzie cut him no slack.

One day, he accompanied McKenzie to the dinner line, and remained in line to chat with him. McKenzie reminded that as an officer, he could go to the front. The Captain responded it was fine, he was OK where he was. McKenzie then stared directly into his eyes and told him he would eat much better if he went to the front.

Puzzled at this, he begged McKenzie to explain. McKenzie responded all would soon become self evident.

On entering, they found the typical sparse servings that were norm for the second wave. McKenzie could see the

Captain's skin tone shading beet red. They sat together (as others from the first wave stared and registered what they felt to be a breach in protocol) and the officer vented how it was a travesty a mess hall would run short during a scheduled meal. McKenzie responded this was the daily norm, even worse on weekends. The Captain stared, now at a complete loss for words. Until hearing that, he had been certain what he witnessed was a single occurrence. McKenzie returned one of his Mona Lisa smiles, adding the Captain was eating what for McKenzie was standard fare, then invited him to town that evening, for some real food. He promised he knew a few good places.

From that point, the good Captain made it his habit to stand in line with the enlisted personnel. McKenzie enjoyed their moments together, and once asked if he was getting used to his lighter weight. The Captain only responded he would not eat better than those he served with. McKenzie liked that. He liked the Captain, and because he liked the Captain, he liked the Marines. In the future, whenever military connivance allowed, McKenzie maneuvered his way into Marine ops. They were his adopted family, cut from the same fabric.

But, we digress.

During that period, it was McKenzie's practice to take late afternoon distance runs before settling in for evening studies. He eventually found and explored wilderness trails winding through the peninsula hilltops above the base. He enjoyed the solitude of running through wilderness and frequently encountered the indigenous animals, notably the half sized deer of the locale. These magical moments lifted his spirit. It was his practice to do this in all weather, even on those winter evenings where rain was so thick a runner could disappear into a curtain of water, and not be seen by anyone else.

On one such occasion, he did his warmups in a grove of trees overlooking the cafeteria. At first everything looked to be normal. Then he noticed some members of the staff, in fact, the noncom and his three cronies, coming out the back as several cars lined up. Next thing, they loaded the vehicles with what appeared to be meat, and frozen food product. McKenzie's rage emerged even before he pieced together the meaning of what he witnessed. He had an instinct for dissemblance, and sometimes smelled it before he knew for sure it was there. He carefully noted all he saw, then continued on his way, trying to weigh its significance, and his plays.

Afterwards, he timed his jaunts carefully, witnessing the same behavior several times each week. He could almost predict when it would occur, and marveled that MP's would drive by the scene routinely, and not register anything. So too would other officers and administrators doing their evening jogs and walkabouts.

Like a lot of folks, McKenzie learned to adjust to life's challenges on the fly. By then, he had become content with walking, or riding his motorcycle into town for his real meals. On one of those forays, he hooked up with the Captain and asked how his diet was holding up. The Captain had discovered Dennys and Sambos and responded things were looking better. Good food, good price, good coffee.

McKenzie decided to share the whereabouts of his secluded jogging trail, knowing the officer believed in conditioning, but would also be observant. He made sure to add, "You'll see all sorts of interesting things back there."

His friend stared quizzically, McKenzie covered his mouth with both hands like the Chinese monkey speaking no evil, "You'll figure it out when you see it."

At some level, McKenzie wished it had been he who made it all come together. It wasn't meant to be. Like most, he was simply trying to survive and get by. He had not yet evolved into a man of decisive and immediate action.

Not long afterwards, there was a combined military and civilian police raid on the cafeteria, and an overnight change in personnel. Subsequently, menus improved dramatically.

They never talked further to the issue, except the Captain continued to join McKenzie's once disadvantaged spot in the food line. Food servings improved to everyone's relief and benefit.

McKenzie once asked him why he continued to enter from the rear. The officer responded that earning the right to the front means knowing first what is happening in the rear, and ultimately that's where leadership skills were nurtured.

Words to ponder.

The Captain and McKenzie remained friends, and in time, came to share several adventures. They ultimately parted ways, each taking his own fated life path. He felt to always remain in the good Captain's debt for a life lesson learned. Over the years, as he continued his own growth and transformation, McKenzie took care to emulate the Captain's fine example. Stand with the people who drive the engine, see that every last person gets their due, and never step over those whom you are committed to serve.

McKenzie's Place

This time, Morrison got better than he bargained for.

In a society without classes, Henry or "Hank" was royalty of the first order. At one time or another, his face sprayed across the cover of every major news weekly. His name crystallized the American ideal of "Success." Big Business first crowned Hank Morrison as their "wunderkind" when he emerged as the fulcrum in history's five largest corporate takeovers. He excelled at finding asset laden, debt ridden takeover targets, then turning those acquisitions into hard cash.

Though famous as a raider, his biggest coup came long after he abandoned the buyout scene, and inherited control of Corridor Airlines from his late father. Corridor started long before as a commuter airline, serving the business needs of the northeast corridor. Initially, for Morrison, it was little more than a diversion. By the third annual report, the "hobby" had grown into a major force in an otherwise tightly competitive market. Average flight occupancies of 91%

made the publicly held corporation one very cash rich prospect for takeover.

That realization soon came to Morrison's former cronies, now representing the interests of United World, the nation's largest passenger carrier. United, a cash poor monolith, reckoned it could take over the smaller airline, absorb its flight schedules, and siphon off its cash to upgrade United's mother fleet into the next decade. Not to mention the generous bonuses and lucrative stock options for those who pulled it off.

Morrison called it the "Philadelphia Shuffle." The folks at United World thought he was bluffing. Before the machinations became public, United had already scheduled a press conference to announce their "friendly" acquisition of Corridor Airlines. Phase two, already scheduled to follow, meant replacing Hank Morrison as Chairman of the Board and CEO. After a consolidation board meeting, United would announce its blueprint for integrating both airlines.

The meeting never came. Morrison's "Philadelphia Shuffle" meant that cash rich Corridor, through a nefarious stream of stock acquisitions, had already garnered controlling interest in the unsuspecting United, and was now in the driver's seat. Morrison summarily dismissed his former compatriots, he could not forgive treachery, especially from old friends. To further prick their wounds, Morrison refused to authorize any compensation for their efforts, arguing they failed to produce the Corridor acquisition, per their original terms with United.

As his hobby, Morrison used Corridor as a vehicle to escape the rat race. Now, he felt trapped. Running what had become the world's largest airline stirred a need to escape unlike any he had known before.

The opportunity arose on his 40th birthday. Characteristically, he rented a seven story brothel in Bangkok, and flew friends in from all corners of the globe to celebrate for seven days. The ultimate blowout! Even his efforts to escape bore the "stamp" of campish extravagance that now associated with his name.

Fortunately, this would be his final escape! There would be no need for others in the future.

While the party lulled, he happened upon a Thai taxi driver, recently returned from a sojourn in a highland monastery. The driver jokingly noticed how he looked much younger than Hank, even though he was, in fact, twenty years older. He spoke true, and Morrison nodded his head in acceptance. He knew the toll on himself. He accepted accelerated aging as a professional malady. But the driver's words cut close and reminded him how he had aged a decade since taking on a little known commuter airline as a "hobby."

Hank thought he'd have some fun with the fellow, "So Khrap[2], how do I undo it all?"

_____

[2] Thai Language for "Sir."

The driver responded it would not be easy, he could see Morrison was a hunter, always on the prowl, sometimes even when there was no prey.

Morrison held silent, surprised at such words from a taxi driver.

"When the hunter is about, nothing is at ease, especially the hunter, whose whole being is focused on the prey. With no prey, the focus is like a burning glass, turned back upon itself."

The driver speculated Morrison needed to "remove himself" from the detrimental influences of his daily life.

"If you want, I can take you to the country. With some luck, you can visit the temple, until you are restored."

Though he hesitated, and struggled with the proposal, Hank really had no alternative. Returning to his quarters in Bangkok, he quietly made the arrangements, in the end, hiring the driver to act as his chauffeur and guide. After making the necessary calls, they headed north. First, they crossed the rice plains of the lower delta. Fish were purchased from the local peasants. Then, they sidetracked among the ancient ruins of Ayutiah, where Morrison paid a herder $2.00 for the privilege of photographing some water buffalo. Further north, they explored the monkey village. Here Buddhist monks perpetuated the practice of nurturing the animals from which the village took its name.

They overnighted in Udorn, then traveled still further north, eating a late breakfast at the bazaar in Nong Kai.

Across the Mekong stood the Laotian capitol of Vientiane, which the driver explained, was little more than an outpost for brigands.

The cab then took a westerly course along a primitive jungle road, until the road ended at the base of an immense wall, imprinted with swirling lines. Morrison walked behind the driver, following him around the wall. Passing from the brush, the driver fell to his knees in prayer. Morrison surveyed the scene, and found that he was standing before an immense statue of the Buddha, reclining like a huge fallen tree on the jungle floor. Far to the left, he saw its head propped comfortably on folded hands. The cab sat parked by the Buddha's feet, far to the right. It was the soles of the feet which had been the immense wall.

The driver proved to be a good ally. Though Morrison couldn't understand a word that anyone said, those in attendance were obviously comfortable with his presence, judging by their pleasant expressions, and the fact all were focused on his every need. Morrison thought perhaps the driver had volunteered promises of largesse to follow.

Had Morrison understood their language, he would have known their smiles had much to do with how unsafe it was for a perfumed foreigner, wearing a silk suit, to be standing at the door of a temple, with nothing but a frail wall separating him from the sex-starved novices inside.

Realistically, his money meant nothing to them. It could buy nothing here. They fed him and washed him, and then, put him up for the night, as they would have done for any human being. These were the people of the northern

41

highlands, and the compassion of Buddha was strong in them.

Morrison found the place to his liking, and had already decided this would be the perfect escape. At his insistence, the driver attempted to make arrangements with one of the saffron-robed monk elders. The elder politely refused, and, had Morrison understood, he would have reacted strongly to the monk's explanation that the temple would be desecrated by turning it into a playground for the rich.

The following day, they were about to leave, when a figure emerged from the distant horizon. As the man animal drew nearer, Morrison recognized the shape of what he took to be a fellow American, sporting the ragged remains of U.S. combat fatigues. The figure slid into clearer focus, a man carrying a 5-gallon water container.

"Thank you God! A fellow American!," Morrison exclaimed.

Mirroring surprise, the figure gawked back, "Thank you Buddha! A fellow American!"

He walked directly up to Morrison, extended his hand and introduced, "Hi! I'm Mason, Mason McKenzie."

"Hank Morrison," shaking hands, "What the hell are you doing here, spying or something?"

Laughing, McKenzie said, "You know friend, that's a question that never gets answered around here, even when it gets answered. No, nothing like that. I had nothing better to do after the war, liked it here, liked the people and the language, so I thought I'd hang around."

"But how do you get by?" queried Morrison.

"Actually, the natives have been very generous," responded McKenzie, not explaining further.

Already thinking ahead, Morrison asked, "Well look, how would you like to make an extra $1000?"

"Who would I have to kill?"

"Nothing of the sort," said Morrison as he counted off ten $100 bills in front of McKenzie. "Just get me into the temple for two weeks."

"Are you on the run or something?" asked McKenzie.

"No, I just need to escape for awhile. You might say I'm coming up for some air."

"Oh, I see," replied McKenzie, "You're here as a student of religion, wanting to research Buddhism," winking an eye with a half smile toward Morrison.

To which Morrison, beaming that he had once again found the right person at just the right time, replied, "Yeah! Whatever it takes," then handed the money over.

McKenzie turned to the cab driver, and gave him the full $1000. "This is to reward you for your kindness to the foreigner. It would be appropriate that you return in two weeks' time to take him back to his revelry in Bangkok."

Facing back to Morrison, McKenzie said, "It's all arranged."

Morrison eventually learned that Mason McKenzie was an abbot at the temple, and stood in charge while the head abbot was on pilgrimage. McKenzie spoke the local tongue, and, for the time being, ran the show.

Morrison felt he had been "conned" out of $1000.00.

Once in the sleeping area, Morrison managed to cool down, "What's the program going to be? Calisthenics at sunrise? Newspapers at eight? Breakfast served till ten?"

McKenzie interrupted, "Up at 4:30 am, do your chores, visit the village with your begging bowl, return to the compound for meditation, eat your daily meal before noon, then report to me at 1:00 pm for further assignment."

McKenzie left.

The jungle's cool evening breath licked the monastery grounds, nearly intoxicating Morrison with the verdant sweetness of life that lingered only as a distant memory.

The next morning, he was awakened by two helpful monks, who escorted him to a local pond. Here, the three cleansed themselves, and readied for the day's activities. By 5:30 am, they stood robed and in line, when, to some silent signal, they moved forward in single file. Wherever

Morrison looked, people waited with their morning food offerings. There was no want of generosity here. Within an hour, they returned to the temple grounds, where each retreated to his own area for morning study. To some, this meant meditation. To others, studying the scriptures. Morrison saw McKenzie walking toward a small group in the distance, doing ritualistic dance like movements, using swords. Tired, Morrison decided to lay down, and soon found himself half asleep, half awake, studying a Gecko glued to the ceiling above him.

Suddenly, the figure of a young monk appeared to his right side.

The monk pantomimed an eating motion. Morrison understood. To his surprise, his watch showed 11:30 am.

Morrison emptied his bowl, knowing the charity of few cultures would have filled the bowl so well.

At 1:00 o'clock, he followed an elderly nun to a large, open air pavilion with a floor of polished teak. Mason McKenzie sat on a mat, centered at the far end, carefully positioned between the two rows of roof supporting columns. The smell of incense wafted in the air, and Morrison saw a wisp of smoke rising from an urn to McKenzie's right.

Somewhat uncomfortable with the surroundings, he gingerly closed the gap to McKenzie, noting, once again, the fatigues.

"Shall we call the $1000 you gave away, my tuition, paid in full?"

"The money was your payment to the driver, for protection provided, and service faithfully rendered, and don't forget his promise to return for you."

Morrison replied, "Don't you think $1000 is a bit exorbitant? Why up here, it's six month's wages!"

"I figured to include the tip," replied McKenzie, a slight grin tracing across his lips.

Compelled to speak last, Morrison responded, "That's fine, so long as you remember that from here on out, there will be a more direct relationship between what I pay and what I receive."

Changing the topic, McKenzie noted "Your tuition here, is what you do for yourself. The food is provided by the locals, you will have your chores, and you will have your lessons. Your free time, is yours to do with as you wish. You might enjoy exploring the surrounding woods, but be on guard for snakes, tigers, mercenaries, drug runners, and bandits." McKenzie winked.

"Lessons? And what might my lessons be?"

Laughing, McKenzie responded, "Well, you're in a temple, don't you think we should try something mystical and esoteric?"

"Such as?"

"Ever read Bali?" queried McKenzie.

"Nope."

"Enjoy chanting?"

"Never tried it, though I do practice TM."

McKenzie frowned.

"Well, maybe you like riddles," said McKenzie, "I mean, all thinking men like riddles."

Morrison's face lit up. "I don't know about riddles, but I love to solve problems. In fact, while I'm here, I can help you folks upgrade your sanitation, lay in a couple more foundations, and roads, I can do..."

McKenzie interrupted. "You will tell me the sound of one hand clapping!"

"What!" retorted Morrison.

"Not this minute," said McKenzie, "You'll have this afternoon to contemplate, but tomorrow at 1:00 pm, we'll meet again to review your answer."

As Morrison took a breath to make what he felt to be a valid protest, McKenzie lifted and rang a small brass hand bell, signaling a young monk to enter. "You must go now. It is Mai's time."

Henry left the covered pavilion, and found a path leading into the jungle. As was his habit, he walked to ease his anger. In his world, people didn't talk to him like that, or treat him so lightly. People respected who he was, or so he thought.

Had there been a way, he would have left the temple now. He had already concluded that nothing constructive could come of this venture.

After walking a bit, he found the jungle broke through to a marshy clearing. In the distance, several men waded in a monsoon fed lake, clapping the surface with their hands. To their front, others, positioned a net to trap any fish escaping the disturbance. Fishing in this manner intrigued Henry, and he decided to watch. As he often said to admiring audiences, the successful entrepreneur starts with insatiable curiosity.

He sat on the bank, close by to the fishermen. After a bit, they curled the net and dragged it to the shore, where Henry discovered they had netted several sizable carp.

One of the peasants, an older man, turned toward Henry, lifting one of the fish with both of his hands. Henry, well defended, thought "Can't I go anywhere without people trying to sell me things I don't need?"

Wearing a big grin, the man walked to Henry's front, and pushed the fish up to his face. Had Henry so desired, he could have counted the rows of scales, up and down, front to back.

Trying to communicate, Henry crossed his hands and waved the peasant off, saying things like "no money", "not hungry", "please, I'm just taking a rest...I'm hiking."

As Henry's hands reached out in gesture, the peasant laid the fish into his palms. Henry instantly felt the life force of the animal, as he stopped mid sentence, and looked eye level at the creature he was holding. Thoughts that couldn't possibly exist in a supermarket fomented in his head. A period of silence passed, and Henry reached out, returning the fish to the peasant with a "No, thank you!"

Washing his hands in the water, Henry elected to return to the temple and work on the riddle. Like the carp he had just seen, he resigned himself that for the moment his own destiny was out of his hands.

The following day, at 1:00 pm, he sat before McKenzie.

McKenzie raised his eyes from the work at hand, smiled, and asked "Tell me what you have learned about the sound of one hand clapping."

Morrison replied, "The question has no answer, one hand cannot clap."

McKenzie, still smiling, said, "The question has an answer. You must find it. Think on it and return at 2:00 pm."

Like any good entrepreneur, Morrison had to consider the possibilities. Possibly, the riddle did have an answer. Hedging his bets, Morrison also allowed for the possibility that McKenzie didn't truly know the answer to the question.

Perhaps, he was nothing more than a burnt out soldier of fortune roosting in this godforsaken forgotten corner of the world, where he occupied a position of minor importance, beyond anything available to him elsewhere.

At 2:00 o'clock, Morrison returned to announce, "I've struggled with this intensely for over an hour, and can think of nothing that could be an answer to your riddle. I need some help. Some guidance."

Morrison, the quintessential negotiator, figured the more he could get McKenzie to say, the more he would know about whether an answer existed in fact.

McKenzie's brow folded into a look of astonishment. "Repeat what you just said!"

"I said that I could think of nothing that might be an answer to your riddle."

"I'm floored. I've never had anyone make such progress in a mere hour's time." McKenzie summoned several robed monks into the pavilion and, in their Thai-Lao tongue, translated the answer he had gotten from Morrison. They all nodded in admiring approval, one even flashing "thumbs up" to Morrison.

Facing Morrison, McKenzie said, "Of course, now I must test your answer. Go ahead and explain it to me."

Morrison stood silently, still replaying what he had just witnessed.

McKenzie, tsk tsk'ing and waving his finger to and fro in front of Morrison said sternly, "An answer without content is not an answer. Come try again at 3:00 pm."

At 3:00 pm, Morrison returned, angry to the point of belligerence. "You could be providing me some guidance. Instead, you give nothing."

The astonished look returned to McKenzie's face for an instant, and then there was silence. "We gave you many clues at 2:00, but other clues are everywhere. Look for them, find the answer."

Morrison returned at 4:00, at 5:00, and again at 6:00. No words were exchanged with McKenzie.

He was starting to dislike McKenzie!

He felt that somehow, McKenzie had gained the edge on him, through some downright slick maneuvering. Even if Morrison wanted to leave, he couldn't. He was stuck in the middle of nowhere, without transportation, and without the ability to communicate. His only tie to civilization would not return for one week and six days.

The following day, and the day after, Morrison became silent. He talked to no one, not even McKenzie. By the end of day three, McKenzie declared Morrison's self imposed "speech fast" would complement his search for the sound of one hand clapping. McKenzie had thought about recommending a speech fast anyway, but held off, convinced his recommendation would have been summarily rejected. Again, McKenzie praised Morrison's instincts.

"But tell me, why did you decide to enter the fast."

Morrison chose not to respond. He focused on his anger, and the fact three days had passed, and somewhere inside lay the sound of one hand clapping. He listened intently, but heard nothing.

On the fourth day, at 1:00 pm, as Morrison entered the pavilion, McKenzie announced, "Let's go for a walk!"

The high ground of the temple stood 1000 feet over the valley, and at its topmost, a small enclosure housed a golden Buddha. The Buddha sat in lotus. Surrounding the Buddha were thousands of bronze bells, which chimed with the slightest breeze. Though Morrison had only seen glimpses of the structure during his walks, the sound of the bells was omni present.

"Your negative thoughts concern me. They impede your efforts to solve the riddle."

Morrison quick-glanced toward McKenzie, and fixed a stare.

McKenzie, averting the gaze, replied, "Your stare means nothing here. I will not let you control me."

"Those are fine words from someone keeping me here virtually as a prisoner," fumed Morrison. His outburst was so contrary to the normal ambiance, the creatures of the surrounding jungle stopped, and listened for more to follow. Even the bells stood silent as the seconds passed, waiting for McKenzie's response.

"On the issue of why you are here, my memory is certain. You came into our midst one day and asked permission to stay. As I recall, you wished to escape. Now you wish to escape again, only you wish to escape back to that which you only just escaped from. I don't know that I understand it. I suspect that your feeling like a prisoner somehow relates to your search for the sound of one hand clapping."

He continued, "So there is no misunderstanding, you must know that you are not prisoner here, just as you are not prisoner in your body, in this world, or in this life. You are free to make your choices. Lest you be unclear as to what they are, I will outline them for you. If you stay, your taxi-driver friend will return on the fourteenth day, to pick you up. If you remain in the temple, you must pay by following the program. For the time being, that means your schedule, and the riddle. That's our contract. I think you can understand that. There are other activities at the temple, but they would be meaningless to you, and of no service to your benefit."

McKenzie continued, "Your other choice is to leave the temple. Then, you would be on your own. You can choose to find your own way back to Bangkok, or to wait till your driver returns. If you choose to stay, you follow the program. If you choose to leave, you make out on your own. You can not choose to stay here, and not follow the program."

"You see! I am a prisoner," cried Morrison. You know damned well I'd be lost if I stepped out the front gate."

"I don't believe that," said McKenzie. "You can do anything."

McKenzie, of course, knew nothing about the "Philadelphia Shuffle," or United World, or the seven story brothel in Bangkok. Well, maybe perhaps the brothel. News of such remarkable indulgences traveled even to the provinces. His statement that Morrison could do anything was an actualization of his own basic belief that man controlled the material world, and not vice verse. He genuinely felt Morrison had the wherewithal to solve the riddle instantly, or to walk out the gate and survive. What puzzled McKenzie was that Morrison resisted both.

"Remember, you chose to be here. You chose to ask the driver; you chose to enter the temple compound; you chose to ask the elder; and you chose to ask me. You know as well as I that if I had said no to your offer of $1000, you would have doubled it to get me to do exactly what I did, and what I would have done for free. If what I speak is false, say so now, and choose to leave. If I am right, you can still choose to leave, or you can choose to stay. But why, when the facts are still clear in our minds, do you choose to re-write history? Why do you choose not to hear the sound of the one hand clapping?"

They neared the shrine of the golden Buddha, and the sound of bells seemed everywhere. Morrison walked straight into the pavilion, where he was instantly lost in sound. It was everywhere. It vibrated in his ears, on his skin, even under his feet.

His sense of vision returned just long enough for him to see McKenzie headed down the trail. McKenzie turned, and waved, as though to say "see you later."

Morrison remained. He could not tell if his eyes were doing anything. There was only the sound. He would step slowly to the right, then to the left. Like being in water for the first time. He looked around to make sure no one else was there, or looking at him. Then he began to move, at first awkwardly, improvising whatever came to mind, trying to blend with what he heard. At times, he stood on one leg, emulating the crane, and then, at other times he fish-swam around the sound-filled chamber. With closed eyes, he circled about aimlessly, even lifting his arms at times as though flying. Time stopped. When finally he opened his eyes, he stood before the sitting Buddha, whose bulbous white eyes stared down its golden nose through black pupils, directly at Morrison. The show was for him. The bells rang, the floor vibrated, and the Buddha stared cross-eyed. No one was doing anything, but it was all for him. It was a wonderful show. No one was doing anything, but it was all for him, he replayed the phrase over and over, until later in the evening, he stumbled down the hill, returning to the compound laughing in the darkness.

On day six, at the third session, Morrison entered the pavilion with a deep grin painted across his face, announcing, "I've got it!"

McKenzie, jokingly responded, "Then you'd better not come too close."

Morrison said, "Watch!"...and he began to swing his hand wildly through the air, sometimes scribing circles, sometimes figure eights. Can you hear it Mason?"

"I wish I had a camera," McKenzie replied, "There are a lot of your former associates who would pay to see this. Take a second and explain to me what you are doing."

"This is the sound of one hand clapping," he said. "Obviously, it can't be clapping against another hand. If it's to generate sound, it must be clapping against something, therefore, it's clapping against the molecules of air. Can't you hear it?"

"Yes!" replied McKenzie, "That is a reasonable answer, albeit incomplete. Now, quickly, take out the reason, what does that leave you with?"

Morrison stopped, McKenzie glared at him, "Quick! You almost have it!... Say it!... Now!"

Morrison was empty, but he could not act.

McKenzie's next words cut sharply through the empty silence. "Enough for today. Return tomorrow."

Morrison was stuck. He was no closer to the answer, but now his mind filled with images. No one was making it happen, but it was all for him. He had chosen it all.

That night, he didn't sleep. He couldn't. He wondered why the golden Buddha sat with crossed eyes. Why did a 15th century artist see Buddha as having crossed eyes?

Next morning, he walked with eyes crossed, as he made the morning rounds for food. It reminded him of being on the "speech fast," but he could not see a clear connection. He was certain that within there was one hand clapping, and there was a sound, but how was it possible to get to where the sound was? Without...without what?

It was now day nine. On this occasion, Morrison found McKenzie in the courtyard. He followed McKenzie out to the athletic yard, where advanced students practiced what McKenzie called the "animal movements." It was a way of moving, a way of centering, a way of self defense.

"Maybe the problem is that you're too cavalier in your approach," said McKenzie.

Suddenly, McKenzie turned toward Morrison and announced, "While you slept, the elders and I met, and we decided that if you fail to solve the riddle, you will be put to death at noon on the fourteenth day."

Silence followed. Morrison studied the warrior monks as thoughts flashed about how he had stumbled onto some hidden cult, and now the cat was finally coming out of the bag.

Checking himself, he turned toward McKenzie and asked, "Is that the truth?"

McKenzie laughed, "No! We don't do that! But, the example speaks for itself. How different would your search for the answer be if you knew you had only five days of life remaining? Or, if I told you that in 60 seconds you would be dead unless you produced the sound of one hand clapping?"

McKenzie's voice trailed off into the distance. Morrison followed McKenzie's words, but for now, the words drifted meaningless onto a sea of sound.

Later that day, he came to McKenzie, "I think I'm onto something."

McKenzie glanced, inquisitively.

Morrison reached forward with his right hand, and sharply slapped McKenzie's left cheek.

There was quiet, expectation swelled within Morrison.

"You should never touch another person, unless you first get that person's consent," McKenzie, looking sternly, continued, "Some within the temple would have considered that a green light for martial arts practice."

Addressing the issue at hand, McKenzie added that, "Your answer went beyond reason, and was a manifestation of pure logic. I asked you for the sound of one hand clapping."

Morrison interrupted, "That's exactly what I gave you. What you heard when my hand struck was the sound of one hand clapping."

McKenzie finished his thought, "...and what you gave me was the sound of one hand clapping against the side of

McKenzie's head. Of course, through careful application of logic, one might argue that what you gave me is the answer. But I am not interested in conclusions of logic, or the arguments supporting them. Your task is to give me the actual sound of one hand clapping. Take the side of McKenzie's head out of it." Stop thinking about it, and do it, time is short."

"You don't like me, do you?" queried Morrison.

McKenzie rolled his eyes skyward, thinking to himself that logic and reason were like trapped rats. As you move closer to remove them from your home, or from the home of a friend, they're capable of emitting terrifying screams, and, when most tightly cornered, they attack to the front. This man, whom Buddha had entrusted to his care for but a fragment of time, had progressed to the point that logic and reason had now targeted McKenzie for a last ditch frontal assault.

He would have to be very clever!

Morrison went on, "And so, people like me are busting our asses turning sow's ears into purses, finding jobs for hundreds of thousands of people, while dropouts and malcontents like you, who couldn't make it in the real world, set yourselves up like little Bodhisattvas, riding herd on a bunch of superstitious peasants who don't know any better..."

McKenzie's right hand moved slowly out from the center of his body, his palm facing outward, signaling firmly for Morrison to stop talking.

"Leave!" McKenzie ordered.

First, a period of silence, then Morrison continued, "Not in your goddamned life! I've paid my dues, and I've earned my say, even if it means I have to walk out the front door to wander barefoot through the jungle for the next couple of days."

McKenzie, taking charge, interrupted, "Sow's ears to purses. What the hell does that mean?"

"It means that my purpose for being on this planet is to take whatever I find, no matter how worthless, and to make it better."

"And who is to judge that a sow's ear, once it has become a purse, is better?"

"The person who needs the purse does!"

"And what the hell does the sow think about it? What would you say if I told you that last month, I had a pig in front of me, trying to convince me that he was making the world a better place by converting worthless Morrison ears into purses? If it weren't for my convincing him otherwise, today you'd be sitting here with gaping holes in the sides of your head, trying to read my lips!"

Both men stopped for an instant, to consider the image that McKenzie had set forth, then broke into a joint fit of laughter. McKenzie pumped his lips like a puppet as though he were talking, indeed, a gifted mime, which only brought tears to the unhearing Morrison's eyes. As his fit of laughter climaxed, his anger was gone.

McKenzie continued, "The point, my friend, is that it is one thing for the pig to find some Morrison ears lying useless on the sidewalk, which he takes home and refines to purses. It is quite another thing when Mr. Pig breaks into our pavilion from out of the jungle, with an axe destined for the side of your head. The people who buy purses know only that somebody gets the materials somehow. But, the "Morrison" soon learns he can no longer walk the jungle paths, for between the greedy pigs, and their cronies, there is no peace. Just fear! Make a note of that comment, because the path to peace is the sound of one hand clapping. Of course, whatever it is that drives Mr. Pig doesn't stop there. To make his activity acceptable to the purse buyers, and to the occasional protestors, he'll lobby that, at considerable additional expense to himself, he has decided to incorporate anesthesiology into the ear removal process so that the "Morrison" suffers less when its ears are being severed. Thinking as a business person, it would only be a matter of time before Mr. Pig discovers when Morrison ears run low, he can substitute McKenzie ears, taxi driver ears, or even peasant ears, and no one will ever know the difference.

"Imagine a redwood tree at the turn of the century, imperial in its age and its majesty, cut down, and made into figurines and furniture, with the remnants turned into scrap wood. To the entrepreneur, the finished items, figurines and furniture are truly beautiful and unique in their own right, and by his labor the craftsperson has 'enhanced' the 'value' of the tree. Perhaps he even advanced the human experience by adding to the cumulative total of art in existence. The craftsperson's skills will be commensurately rewarded. Now, think what remains of the redwood. The scraps, the chips and the splinters. Because they had no "use" they were simply disposed of, perhaps even put to the fire. Ask yourself! Do any of the end products stand up to the redwood in its original state?

"Reason is to truth, as the carved figurines and scrap are to the original redwood. The person who knows truth, knows the redwood, and his first question must be, 'What is best for the tree?' The voice of reason will ask 'What is best for me, and then the person who will buy the figurines?' If Mr. Pig had asked me whether I wanted a purse made from Morrison ears, I would have answered that I want Morrison and his ears as one. I want the sound of one hand clapping. The sound of one hand is the sound of truth, not the sound of reason."

Morrison had no response. He tried to recapture everything McKenzie had said, and feared he had already lost bits and pieces. He stood motionless while McKenzie bowed and left the pavilion.

Morrison would have much to contemplate that evening.

By the following day's session, Morrison believed the riddle had a specific answer. He felt it inside himself, and he felt it outside himself, but he could not find the words to express it, or the images to define it.

During the days following, McKenzie had commented more than once about how Morrison looked like a constipated child and, while saying it, McKenzie's face would grow into the most grotesque distortions, manifesting maximum, but unproductive intestinal effort.

On day thirteen, the lesson commenced promptly at 1:00 pm with McKenzie's announcement that, "During the war, I was once captured..."

Without words, Morrison signaled his intense interest. McKenzie had hooked him. The story followed.

"It was during the Tet offensive. Our outlying position was overrun. We had taken heavy casualties, when a grenade exploded close by. The shock, or maybe the fear, caused me to lose consciousness. When I awoke, I was on my feet, hands tied behind my back, following a procession of North Vietnamese regulars. How does one explain it except to describe it the way it was? I was happy that the regulars had captured me, because I had seen what undisciplined guerrillas could do to their prisoners.

"They took me to a jungle compound, where my cell was a wooden box. It measured 2 feet wide, by 2.5 feet high, and 3 feet deep. It had no lock on the outside. The front panel slid down from above into pre cut grooves. There was no light, and no holes for air. A #10 coffee can served as my bathroom.

"The first several hours were an eternity. Though I never saw any of them, I heard other prisoners screaming, and banging against the walls of their boxes. Some even broke down into infantile howling. What was most curious, is that only one person did this in English. Me!

"Thinking of it now, I can visualize some deity watching from far above, listening to the comi-tragic opera being transmitted in Korean, Vietnamese, Cambodian, Lao, Chinese, and English from the planet below. Many voices...one dreadful tune.

"Though it cut off everything my human nature needed to exist, it wasn't long before I adapted to the box. Some people didn't. Whenever the panel opened on an adjoining box, I would listen carefully for sounds of life nearby. Once, when I heard the sound of a lifeless body being pulled from its container, I found myself unable to breathe. It would no longer come naturally. From that point, I had to "will" myself to take each breath...always, mind over matter.

"In time, I assessed the situation, using reason, and my capacity to think. I found myself learning how to be comfortable in the box. After a week, I no longer even questioned whether I could survive. Rather, I was concerned about the number of cheeseburgers and milkshakes I would order when I finally returned stateside.

"Then, I lost track of time. I simply didn't care about it anymore. Once, one of the guards let me out to stand in the moonlight (they would never allow me to view the camp in daylight). He laughed at my taking cupped hands and carefully sweeping out the interior of my 'home,' before I back-entered into it. As the front panel slid closed, my hand felt a soft leathery globe on the floor of the box. Though I couldn't see it, I recognized it immediately as an orange. It was a precious gift, for an orange was a priceless commodity to all sides in this war.

"I spent another eternity, carefully savoring every fiber of the precious fruit. Though I hadn't seen the sun since the day of my capture, I could feel its chemistry within me as the life giving serum hit on switches throughout my body.

"To my dismay, weeks turned to months. The camp took its cumulative toll. I found I was becoming weak. My anticipated release was now a distant, unfulfilled hope, locked in the past. At some point I recognized my death was near. My only choices were to escape, or to perish. I could no longer choose to wait, and expect to survive.

"One day, I was awakened by the sound of a body being dragged from its box nearby to the right. When the time came for evening stretch, my guard 'friend' nodded toward the body, and shook his head. I looked at his face. In it, I saw brothers gone, sisters prostituted, and children maimed. The war had become old for him. In the distance, I saw two silhouettes, dragging other bodies toward an open pit. The powdered lime in the pit gleamed white, like snow, in the moonlight. How ironic, for me the pit was simply another box, just bigger.

"When I re-entered my box, I saw that for once, the front panel was not closed shut. Checking my perception, I ran my fingers beneath it. It was true! Had I a mind to, I could lift it!

"I kept pressure against the panel, cautious not to let it drop completely shut. I listened everywhere. When your life depends on it, you can hear everything. Several hours passed, and I knew from the sounds that only two guards were patrolling the compound. There were no lights. To have lights in that situation would have been sure suicide for my captors, given the nightly flyovers by B-52's. I lifted the panel slowly, and peered out from my cavern. The sky sparkled with stars, and the moon beamed in its first quarter. I thought, 'Be patient, Mason, don't rush this'...as I lay prone, carefully letting my senses adjust to the surroundings. Astonished, I saw there were no fences, and no perimeter concertina wire. The only prison was our boxes, isolation, and the authority of the armed guards. I moved out without breathing, to a point behind my box, where I had a straight path to the jungle. Though I expected trip wires, land mines, or secondary guards along the perimeter, there were none. My escape was clean, until a sudden terrifying thought came over me. What would happen to my 'friend' if they discovered my empty box in the morning! I was seized with an urge to return to the box. Not to become a prisoner again, but rather to solve the riddle of how to protect my protector. I sat quietly along the perimeter, trying to see a solution, when suddenly, it occurred to me, no one keeps tally of the dead. Once gone, out of the game!

"The body from the adjoining cell lay uncovered atop the lime pit. With reckless abandon, I walked upright into the camp. I can remember even now, thinking that so long as I felt I was invisible to the two guards, they would not notice me. but if I allowed my concentration to lapse for even an instant, they would discover me, and I would be next in the pit.

"I succeeded! I was truly invisible. After dusting off any residue of lime, I placed the body into my box. The ruse was complete. The second time I left the camp, I walked upright, the way a free man should. Would the ruse work? I only wish I could have seen my friend's face the following day. Would he know of my concern for his safety? Would he understand what I had risked to protect him?

"Then again, did I understand what he had risked to protect me? In any event, I never saw him again!

"Well, I didn't know it immediately, but the experience tilted my values onto a new axis. Eventually, I returned to my unit, and eventually, I got home. But, what was once North for me, had become South, and West, East. Afterwards, no matter where I went, or what I did, I still felt like I was in the box. Now don't get me wrong, I'm not saying that I felt like I was back in the camp. Rather, I was forever in a box, as though, no matter what I did, it would end with me in the fetal position and the door sliding shut. Later, I went to school, became a "professional" and, you might be surprised to hear this, was quite successful, at least as measured by the number of "purses" I was able to produce.

"Still, my thoughts always returned to that eternity, which was the first several hours that I spent in the box, when suddenly, like a rocket blasting off from somewhere behind my naval, spiraling up my spine, there was a clear and true voice which screamed that, 'Human beings are not meant for this!' It was a voice I had never heard before. After all, I was too busy with schedules, with counts, with the next things I had to do to get promoted, with making sure that my paycheck got directly deposited to my bank, or with the number of hamburgers I would eat when I finally got home. Long after that, the voice remained, and became stronger.

"Human beings are not made for this, why have you made this your choice?' Whether I was staying up all night cramming for an exam, synthesizing a new marketing strategy, or lying in the sack with a beautiful woman, the question was always there. Everything I was doing was alien to the voice within, which unremittingly reminded that human beings were not meant to be doing what I was doing, then queried why I had chosen to do it."

"Then why did you?" asked Morrison.

"The point is, I hadn't chosen anything. I was conditioned 'not to choose.' I was trained to think so that I wasn't really thinking, to strive for goals that really weren't goals; like a tree growing upside down. Up until my day of awareness, I was so busy plowing over my goals that even while I thought I was gaining control of my destiny, I was losing it completely. I had damned myself. I had been everywhere, but was nowhere. I was a success, but was empty. I was a scholar, but could only think within the box that others, no different than myself, but at another level, had erected for me."

"And, did they know that they had done this to you?"

"Of course not! Like me, they had no awareness. They didn't have the capacity to choose to do anything to me. Their goals were plowed over too! Their being was reduced to maintaining the status quo, keeping me controlled in a box. The more they could see I was properly confined, the less they could see of their own identical predicament."

Morrison playfully wondered whether McKenzie was in fact, describing some variation of the "Philadelphia Shuffle." Who was the perpetrator? Who was the victim?

"So what does it all mean?" asked Morrison.

"It means," said McKenzie, "that we have fallen from grace, that we are exiled from the Garden of Eden, that we no longer remember who we are, or where we came from, or the power that we have over our own existence. We stand satisfied with a universe of boxes, within boxes, our measure of success is merely how able we are to step from one box, into the next one up. And so long as we don't step out, the system remains intact!"

"But you said you had your day of awareness...?" asked Morrison.

"Yes, that's true..." said McKenzie, "The day came when the voice no longer questioned."

"What happened?"

"The sound of one hand clapping! For me, it was the beginning of truth. From that day, I was free to choose. Whatever confronted me, I immediately recognized what was true, and what was not. I could choose either, but the consequences of my choice would belong only to me. That's why you came here. That's why you found me. That's why you stayed. You know now that there is an answer, but you have to get it out. If you don't, you may as well be dead. You may as well be in the pit reserved for the prison compound corpses. This is not a threat, but your survival, or should I say, the survival of what is essentially you, depends on your finding that answer tomorrow. If you don't do it tomorrow, you may never have another chance!"

Morrison had much to contemplate. Instinctively, he glanced at his watch, only to remember that he had stopped wearing it more than a week ago.

"Time's not the same out here, is it?", asked McKenzie, smiling lightly at Morrison.

In response, Morrison lightly shook his head side to side, answering, "No, when I don't think of it, it's not important at all."

McKenzie reached across the space separating them and put his right hand onto Morrison's left shoulder, "Your instincts are good, when you don't think about them. Don't worry so much about the sound of one hand clapping. It's merely the cherry on top of the sundae. With or without it, the sundae is just as delightful."

McKenzie stood, bowed to Morrison, then left the pavilion.

Suddenly tired, Morrison lowered his body to the teak floor, and closed his eyes. He wondered, "Why could the sound of one hand clapping be a matter of life and death one moment, and then the cherry on top of the sundae the next? It just didn't make sense. It couldn't make sense. If it couldn't make sense, why did he waste his time thinking about it? Still, something was happening. It was as though his body, and his senses, perhaps even his 'instincts' as McKenzie had suggested, were close to understanding a basic reality that was beyond the capacity of his reason. He could argue why the sound of one hand clapping would be a matter of life and death, and he could probably just as convincingly argue why it might be considered the cherry on top of the sundae, but if he argued both points simultaneously, he came across as a fool. In the realm of reason, the perceptions were forever to be apart."

Morrison folded his hands in the prayer position, then laid them beneath his right ear, as a pillow.

Outside, the late afternoon rain made its regular monsoonal round. The tapping of the droplets on the tin roof served as a carrier for the "Sa-Ta-Na-Ma" chanting of monks passing outside. Whatever Morrison had been thinking was gone.

The image of the cross-eyed Buddha bubbled slowly forth into his consciousness, the absurdity of its image evoking a broad grin across Morrison's face. He thought, "If I were a cross-eyed Buddha, how would I react to a smiling Morrison statue sitting on top of the hill?"

A comet of insight arched across Morrison's consciousness. It came not as a thought, but as a light, a flashing strobe. "My God, why do I see them as different? Is it possible that the cross-eyed Buddha and the smiling Morrison are one and the same?"

The rain had stopped. Moist jungle aroma poured into the pavilion from all directions. It had become dark. Morrison knew that he had to see the statue one more time before he left. Traversing the hill in the dark might be a bit risky, but this was no time for wanton caution.

It was darker than he thought it would be, the rain clouds and the jungle canopy combined to absorb all light. Fighting his reservations, Morrison glanced upward, where he knew the trail to be, but which, for the moment, was draped in black velvet darkness.

Taking a few tentative steps forward, Morrison veered from the trail, dropping suddenly downward, rolling across the monastery's crop of lemon grass. Though he was stunned, the pleasant lemon odor revived him. When he found his way back to the trail, he threw off his wet and muddied shirt. Facing uphill to the shrine, or downhill to the temple grounds, he saw only the velvet black of night. He felt a breeze from above.

McKenzie had said Buddha taught the world was a place of suffering. The monks learned even though the suffering was real, it was part of who they were, and why they were here. And each of them held the power to stop it all, because in the end, the suffering was their individual load.

Continuing uphill, Morrison struggled with the question of whether his own life could be described as one of suffering.

"Hardly, when compared to that of a leper..."

And no sooner had Morrison thought the thought, then from the same well sprang the question "And if the world measured success by one's leprosy, what would the successful leper think of the plight of the suffering Morrison."

The question slammed into Morrison with such force that his body lifted completely from the ground. He felt himself descending, not so much falling, but floating, like a leaf spinning downward from an autumn branch.

And as the leaf touched the ground, Morrison returned to his reality, which was that of a 200 pound, 40 year old man, falling face first onto the sloping jungle floor.

Morrison's face left its mark on the soft undergrowth. Lying prone, he delicately lifted to his hands and knees, cursing his inattention to the hazards of the darkened trail. He was wet and soiled, and his head was ringed with pain from the crack it sustained. Morrison tried to lift to his feet, but couldn't. It was as though a great weight sat on his shoulders, freezing his body, leaving only his thoughts free to move.

He could scarcely breathe, as he rose to hands and knees, a cauldron of thoughts bubbled over with images of what his life had come to represent. Kneeling motionless, he stood as judge, jury, victim, and oppressor. He had become slave to the cycle of life and death. He struggled further with the pain as he slowly rose to his feet, stepping forward, foot by foot, knowing that he would rest at the top.

Would that he could drop this unnatural load, and be forever unburdened.

Taking a few more steps, he fell once again to his knees. A break in the clouds was visible in the tropical canopy, and, in the starlight, he saw the silhouette of the shrine a short distance away. But, to his immediate front, what seemed like a vine growing upward from the jungle floor, swayed ever so slightly.

A voice inside whispered, "Cobra!"

Had he come this far to turn back!

"No," he would continue, "Cobra be damned!"

And as he stepped forward, what was cobra, was gone, as was his burden.

Turning to look back, he saw that he had passed beyond the darkness.

A cool breeze ran its fingers like a comb along the hilltop, and the sound of bells signaled Morrison's destination.

He entered the shrine and immediately fixed his gaze onto the crossed eyes of the golden statue. Even in the subtle starlight, the statue had a light of its own.

No longer tired, Morrison regretted he would be leaving the next day. He was tied forever to the role his life had become. McKenzie had said, "It is your Karma. But remember, when you are ignorant, a mountain is a mountain. When you are aware, a mountain is something other than a mountain. But, when you are enlightened, the mountain can be a mountain once again."

To which Morrison had replied, "Then why bother with all this? What purpose does it serve?"

McKenzie responded that, "The purpose is merely to still the water. Only then is the ship free to leave port."

A veil of silence passed over the pavilion. All became still.

Morrison sat before the Buddha, eyes drooping from tiredness, cross-eye to cross-eye. In the trance like state preceding sleep, he finally sensed the secret of the statue.

On the other end of time, a native craftsman had dedicated a lifetime perfecting the technology which produced a perfect statue of bronze, albeit with crossed-eyes. He meant to share a vision with his counterpart on the other end of time's tunnel. The craftsman was Morrison from before. He was the craftsman today. The passage of time was merely a wave traversing a sea which remained essentially unchanged.

There was nothing left to consider, only to experience.

The warm sun of dawn wakened Morrison with a casual caress. McKenzie was sitting nearby, waiting patiently in lotus. Seeing that Morrison had awakened, he asked, "Shall we finish what we started?"

Morrison's eyes rose slowly upward as he moved into his own version of lotus across from McKenzie. The cross-eyed Buddha stared down at both, a slight smile passing across its face. McKenzie stared at Morrison, knowing that only reason kept their true natures apart.

Morrison was empty of distraction.

McKenzie looked across, "Then tell me Morrison. What is the sound of one hand clapping?"

Morrison's eyes held McKenzie's stare. From somewhere in the universe, a small thread looped around the wrist of Morrison's right hand. As Morrison held stare with McKenzie, an unseen hand pulled that cord, and lifted Morrison's right arm up and forward, his five fingers pointing straight at McKenzie. McKenzie, knowing the experience, recognized the response. Morrison was dumbfounded.

"And what is the sound of one hand clapping when you are sitting on a stool atop of Everest?"

And again, Morrison's right hand extended up and outward, only this time with a bit more impetus in its thrust toward McKenzie.

"And what is the sound of one hand clapping before you were born?"

This time, Morrison vigorously thrust his hand out with a scream of affirmation.

In concert, the wind blew its own chorus energizing the bells of the shrine.

"And what is the sound of one hand clapping when you are dead?"

Morrison again thrust his hand out to McKenzie.

"How is that?"

Again, Morrison thrust his hand out, exclaiming, "That is how!"

McKenzie, stared through Morrison's eyes, deep into his soul, "But you are dead!"

"No! Not dead. Not alive, but not dead."

Next, only the bells spoke, as the cross-eyed Buddha affirmed.

McKenzie, looking across at Morrison, finally spoke, "I will miss you Mr. Morrison."

Morrison could only nod.

"The monks left you a bottle of rice wine as a present. They said it was to convey their enjoyment in watching your struggle these past two weeks. Of course, that's their way of keeping you in a box of sorts. Few of them have come to the level of awareness that you've attained today. In any event, your driver has already arrived. It is time to gather your possessions and return to your world."

Morrison looked across at McKenzie, took a deep breath, tried to speak, but couldn't. A tear rolled diagonally across his right cheek. "I did not know that leaving would be so hard."

"Yes. But you will go anyway. The world awaits you. I will meet you at the cab."

There, Morrison was greeted warmly by the driver.

"Sir, I am proud of you. I heard that you did quite well."

McKenzie, dressed in his usual fatigues, again carrying the 5 gallon water bucket, emerged from the woods, as though the vegetation had parted to project the image of a man walking forward. As he drew near, the driver carefully loaded Morrison's possessions into the trunk.

Extending his right hand, McKenzie said, "You almost forgot your watch."

Morrison reached out for the watch, and, as he fitted it on his wrist, noticed the hands had been removed.

Morrison glanced up at McKenzie, whose knowing countenance smiled back. "Sometimes, as is your habit, you will think to look at your watch to see what time it is, and, as you see the watch, you will think of me, and your brief sojourn here."

"And what will you be saying to me when I think of you?" asked Morrison.
I will be saying, "Henry, what time is it really?"

Morrison smiled, as he got into the cab.

He had wanted to reach out the window to shake McKenzie's hand farewell, only he discovered that McKenzie had turned to head back into the jungle. His stare followed the teacher's path for the next several steps, until what was once McKenzie, had returned to being a cluster of vines and branches.

In like fashion, Morrison returned to his world, and just as readily, melted into the jungle of concrete and steel. From that day, he knew a mountain when he saw one.

He wore the watch always.

The old Morrison would have considered the thousand dollars well invested.

Christmas in Port Richmond

Growing up in Port Richmond represented a delicate balance of delight and anguish.

It sits north of center city Philadelphia, and though a residential district, back then, it catered to industry, and served as a transportation hub for the for the Delaware Valley. I don't know if it's the same today, but I would hope not.

Many who lived there stayed. Frankly, it was where they were raised, where parents lived, where children were born, where they worked, and where they spent their free time. Embedded into the surrounds were churches, schools, meeting halls, bars, community centers, factories, railroads, trolley lines, gangs, mummers and syndicates. Tension and demands of daily life imbued every individual's experience. Few expected but all hoped for "happiness" as life's promise. Practically speaking, they anticipated "struggle" and aspired somehow to survive to a retirement without misery. Always was the hope their children would have better lives.

Philadelphia summers were unspeakably hot, and each sweltering morning unblanketed with the attending odor of factories, refined metals, and chemicals floating from smokestacks, furnaces, and dump sites, wafting their butterfly courses until coming to rest on our persons, in our lungs, eyes, and hair, even soiling our newly washed cars as a brazen reminder of our helplessness. Typically, autumn came with crisp air, and the fall winds occasionally brought clear days, when times at the local park would transport us to new worlds, where we frolicked through piles of leaves, and admired the squirrels, as wild an animal as many of us would ever see (and a far cry from summer's roaches and rats).

Winters could be almost as unbearable as summers, with bitter cold running deep into our bones whenever we stepped from the embrace of our homes. Steam radiators, now antiques, provided an unforgettable warmth and comfort not found in my life since. Winter brought illness, and every year we dreaded the flu. In those days, people died from it. Being flat on your back for a week or two was to be expected, even when the doctor made housecalls.

In the midst of winter's freeze came Christmas.

Childhood in the big city was on occasion, magical, once you learned how to move about. This may seem hard to believe, but in those days holiday season didn't start until after Thanksgiving. We all eagerly awaited the arrival of Santa and the Macy's Christmas parade as the formal kickoff to Christmas shopping, and the brief period when the entire inner city transformed to crystaldom, with colored lights, snow, music, wreaths, and pleasantries becoming the norm. As a preteen, I would take the trolley and ride the elevator or subway (when it went below ground) into town. There I explored every inch of Wanamaker's, Gimbels, and Lit Brothers, and surveyed the competing displays of Christmas trains, decorations, trees, and abundance. The possibilities seemed limitless.

Of course, nothing good comes without its price. Lest we thought Christmas too good to be true, truth stared at us hard and cold snapping us quickly back to reality.

Our home was a bakery. My stepfather Eddie was the baker, and my mother Wanda ran the business, along with whatever help from family or friends or short term hires they could elicit during the impossibly busy holiday period. Beneath our hundred plus year old inner city brick home, there was an extensive, historical, basement area, with brick ovens, that ran in seemingly endless dimensions and nurtured the ever beating heart of our family enterprise. Eddie liked to say our house used to be the original German school. Even today, decades afterwards, it is hard for me to recollect my stepfather (I feel more comfortable calling him father for the balance of this piece) sleeping between Thanksgiving and New Years. He would occasionally come up, eat, collapse for an hour, then someone in the bakery would call him back to the next batch waiting to come out. It was no different for my mother, who would waken to customers lined up, knocking on our side (residential) entry door in the pre-dawn, hurling profanities about how they had driven from New York to buy some Polish babka, and needed to get back to their families.

In short, it was a madhouse!

My mother was always careful to decorate the store with a Nativity scene, and copious Christmas lights with banners. Our own home, above and beside the bakery, had to wait. Really, there was no living but for the business during that time. Customers would walk into our living room, sit down on the sofa as if to watch TV, and in Polish or English (the languages of Port Richmond), enter long, seemingly never ending, conversations with myself, my mother, my grandmother, my father, or whoever happened to be there.

Like every family business, the bakery was our lifeboat, and it was sacred. Any semblance of family life, or personal life, or personal interests, disappeared in the shadow of this beast (yes, it was a beast, albeit one which provided for our needs and sustenance).

But as a child, I clung to the revelry of the season, and fixed my dreams and wishes on the magic of the moment, not to mention what I hoped to get on Christmas Day. Tension from our lives and environment mounted throughout the period, and the weeks leading to Christmas meant stress, high emotions, bitter arguments, and cataclysmic fights. On top of all, I faced winter examinations at school, along with the impossible requirements and demands of my teachers all the while expecting to be called into the bakery shop, or down to the bakery because of yet another sudden crisis or simply because everyone else was exhausted to depletion. Typically, as Christmas Day approached, our lives became impossibly grim. In the final week all we could look forward to was that it would all stop on Christmas Day (And then start again, for one final spurt, the several days before New Year's.)

We didn't know family traditions from nothing. Just as everything hit the redline (i.e. the fan), the bio-tachometers spinning in blurred circles with everyone on the verge of coming unhinged, Christmas Eve rolled around. It was undoubtedly the busiest day of the year, with the store packed to overflowing the entire day from 5 a.m. until closing at 11 PM. Even after closing, we would have knocks on the door, and scratches at the bakery windows, for those who still wanted some final treats for their families. Though rarely mentioned or even acknowledged by the local population, many families residing in Port Richmond did not have the means or resources to afford even their Christmas sweets. Those families would show up at the doorstep as we closed 11 p.m. inquiring for any leftovers or "day olds." Of course, there were none, only what we kept for our own enjoyment, for friends and family. Somehow, my mother would find something she could call a leftover or day-old pastry, and for a quarter, provide enough for some of those families. I didn't make much of this, until her passing at age 81, having outlived my father, and almost all of her friends. At her funeral, a woman came to me, shook my hand, and said "I want you to know your mother was good to me and my family."

Christmas Day, positioned well into the mid-Atlantic frigid season, was not infrequently accompanied by a hellacious snowstorm. Even today, I remember well the white Christmases that were part of my youth. These even included genuine blizzards, some starting Christmas Eve, and going all the way through till Christmas morning.

Characteristically, I would attend midnight mass. Churches in the inner city were wonderfully huge monolithic structures, all supported by the extraordinary numbers of Catholic immigrants and their descendants who without exception, loyally participated and supported their parishes. Within a mile of our home, there was Nativity (the Irish parish), our Lady help a Christian (the German parish), and St. Adalbert's (the Polish parish). A bit further was St. Ann's (the Italian parish)...you get the idea. At midnight on Christmas Eve, Nativity, which was my usual choice, celebrated a solemn high mass in the top-level church, and a quick mass in the basement church. Because of the spirit of the season, my choice was usually the high mass, which would run until nearly 2 a.m., after which I would hook up with friends, and traverse through the snow under the winter stars (it was the one evening each year when stars were truly visible). Only when the bitter cold overwhelmed would I would return home to the radiator, where my father and mother were nearby, collapsed on their chairs usually watching Alastair Sims in the last showing of Christmas Carol.

I didn't make much of it in the old days, but my father took the Christmas Carol and its lessons, very seriously. I don't remember him ever going to church, but I do remember he never missed the Christmas Carol. Under his tired breath he would mumble curses at Scrooge, and then silently delight in Scrooge's rebirth at the end. In hindsight, I believe for my father, Scrooge was about possibilities. As long as Scrooge continued to be reborn there was somehow hope for Eddie, and a life that had numbed him to all emotion and human interface, could somehow be righted and restored to full beauty in a flash.

Well, it never did work out that way. The unending demands gradually wore him down, until at the end, little of his essential essence remained to be reborn or restored to anything.

So there they were, motionless, collapsed on the couch watching Scrooge, a slight odor of whiskey hovering. The Christmas tree was not up, and presents were not out.

Every Christmas, as I went to sleep in the early a.m. it looked they were so exhausted, that even Santa would pass over our house, scared into head for safer places, rather than deal with this bleakness.

I went to sleep, not expecting Christmas morning to materialize. When the first rays of morning sun forced me awake, I charged down the stairs and inevitably found a huge and incredibly ornamented Christmas tree, sitting atop the TV cabinet with beautifully decorated presents laid beneath, spilling over onto the floor. I was alone, with the entire living room to myself, and my booty. It would be several hours before anyone budged on the second floor, and my father and mother would come downstairs. Late in the morning, sometimes even afternoon, my father would descend the steps, looking like the ghost of Scrooge himself, three-day beard on his face, several layers of bags beneath his eyes, hair going in all directions at once. My mother would appear nearly simultaneously, literally bloated with exhaustion, wearing her robe, and hoping I remembered to buy something for her. My father would say not a word as he passed me, I, completely absorbed with my menagerie, maneuvering about on the floor. He went into the kitchen, lit another cigarette, turned on the coffee, and remained in the kitchen for several hours, with his coffee, smoking cigarettes, not expecting anything beneath the tree to be for himself. Of course, he wasn't forgotten, he simply chose to be patient in his expectations, and hopes. Not surprisingly, today that trait lives within me.

As a youngster, I believed in Santa Claus well beyond the age when most depose him to the realm of pretence. For those Christmases at home, there would be nothing at 2 a.m. on Christmas morning, and a three-ring circus when I awoke at 6:30. To my young eyes and imagination, it was not humanly possible or even explainable. Only a true spirit of the greatest stature and kindness could have turned this depleted, exhausted, and empty home of Christmas Eve, into the carnival of Christmas morning.

You can see why it was so hard for me to let go of Santa Claus.

Now, they are both long gone, and I haven't been to a midnight mass in decades. Though I don't miss the trials of my early childhood in Philadelphia, I never forget that even in their midst irreplaceable blessings were had. To this day, when I am asked by children whether there is a Santa Claus, I respond "Oh yes. And how I miss him, and his helper."

Part 2 - Evolution

The Riddle of Okano

What most I remember is first standing across from Okano. Our eyes met then locked. His were ice, thru which silvery veil lay emptiness.

It was I who issued the challenge, he nodded, grunting an affirmation, asking, "Where? When?"

"The field beyond the pagoda, we'll start as the setting sun touches the horizon, on the day of the full moon." He nodded then left.

Springing this trap proved simpler than anticipated. This would be my day! Vanquishing Okano promised to assure my wealth and prestige for years to come.

My plans were many, I had already scoped and studied the terrain and the conditions of light, I would approach from a direction guaranteeing advantage to myself. Every possibility was weighed and considered, there would be no miscalculations on my part.

He was there as agreed, back turned to me as I arrived, oblivious to my machinations, and clearly ignorant of my plan to steal the advantage. I stopped a respectful 10 paces away, then drew my weapon and waited. He turned about, carefully setting down his rice and chopsticks then casually lifted his weapon, letting its sheath drop on its own from the blade, as he positioned across from me.

I thought to myself, "Has he no respect for his weapon, or its maker?"

But then, just as quickly, another thought emerged. This was all wrong! Where was my hoped-for advantage, my assurance of victory? He stood before me unassailable, but looked no different than any other swordsman of past encounter. What was I missing?

I froze, unable to move, sensing his unfathomable skill and feeling his energy closing like a shadow reeling in the distance between us.

As the shadow's web enveloped me, all burned deep and hot within, even while its eclipse blanketed my agony. My spirit stood locked within this fiery prison, I, the dragon's meal soon to be.

Everything on which I planned to rely thawed into uncertainty. What remained left to actualize my strategy, as I stood exposed and helpless at the precipice?

Why did I ever throw the challenge? When is enough, enough? How could I have failed to see this?

Time stopped as I drifted without hope into his gaze, uprooted and torn from reality.

Eventually I broke, no longer able to stand, I crumbled to the ground and submitted. The full moon glimmered over the the pines. Nausea erupted, held in check only by my locked jaw.

I expected nothing but death. It's what I would have served to my opponent. It's what I deserved.

He stood motionless for what seemed an eternity, then turned about and left, leaving no words.

I expected ridicule and ruin on returning to town, my life as a warrior and protector surely ended, I would be nothing more than a ronin, left to wandering and catering to the vices of thugs and gangsters for sustenance.

As it turned out, he had said nothing, told no one. In fact, he had not even returned to the town.

Those who had wagered pressed me for a full account. At first, I gave no report, my inner shame unbearable. Finally, I told them to seek out Okano, he would give them what they sought (as perhaps he had to me).

Several months afterward, travelers found Okano's body in a remote woods. He had been killed, apparently by a savage beast. I like to think it was a bear, or perhaps a tiger, or both. Nothing less would account for the terrible wounds reported.

But it posed a riddle, to which I have yet to find an answer.

Was not Okano able to effect his enormous power and influence over the beasts, as he had done with me?

Is it possible the beasts did not know how much I knew about what Okano could do?

Crap Eaters

By way of orientation let's briefly recall Ulysses of mythological fame. You recollect Ulysses was famous for his single minded devotion to Penelope, his long suffering wife. After the Trojan War, Ulysses wandered at sea twenty years. He faced legendary challenges from creatures, gods, demigods, tempests and sirens. Only after passing thru this gauntlet did he attain the crowning achievement of his single minded purpose, a return to his home and family.

How much simpler would his life have been without the obstructions and interference of the gods? The diversions from his life's purpose were innumerable and nearly insurmountable. Even then, not everything could be blamed exclusively on the gods or fate. It's clear that failures on the part of Ulysses and his crew, particularly when it came to resisting temptation, contributed every bit as much to their delays, distractions and suffering. Ultimately, the crew was lost. Only Ulysses made it home. There's much to think about in the story, particularly as regards the consequences of foolishness.

The lure of sirens and the wrath of gods are powerful distractions indeed. Still, there exist other equally potent distractions. They hover nearly invisible just beyond our awareness, insidious, barely detectable while stripping our capacity to be fully human.

That brings us to Laughing Jou.

In the north country, Old Jou was a recognized master. He was often sought out by others on the path, and was revered and emulated by all.

But he was not an easy man to figure out, or to get along with.

Generally, his presence was announced by streams of loud and boisterous laughter. Just as certainly, laughter billowed forth when he addressed the seemingly endless questions put to him by others, which to Laughing Jou, represented the squeals of drifting souls mired in darkness. Many thought it impolite. They told him so to his face. It made him laugh all the harder.

He did not tolerate fools. When questioned why people still sought him as they did, he answered (laughing), "Because I am awake," adding, "And because I am so damn patient!" Typically villagers would corner old Jou in the town centers. In the older villages and the outland cities, town center was usually the spot where all incoming arterials met and connected. Most often, there would be a circle and a gathering place in the middle, where commerce might transact, or folks could get together and talk. They could find him in places like this. They would sit eagerly around him, hoping to glean kernels of knowledge, perhaps enough to get a handle on their own struggles with the many questions of existence.

"How can I become like you?" they would ask, "Centered and unaffected by the trials and mishaps of life."

"There's nothing to become."

"How is that so?"

"All you have to do is flush the toilet. Then questions like this will stop pestering you."

"Flush the toilet? We don't get it?"

"What I'm saying is, you're a crap eater. Empty yourself of the crap. You'll find you're better off without it!"

"Crap eater?".

Laughing Jou always found the exchanges hilarious. He meant their thoughts were no different than shit floating around in their heads, stinking everything else up.

When still on the path, I can remember encountering him in the village center. We used to go to him for medicine and divinations, but most of all for the answers to our own incessant questions. He was far more learned than I, or anyone else I knew. I remember one particular exchange above all the others.

Mind you, he was a formidable and imposing presence despite his ever present good humor. Typically, as villagers timidly approached, the master would sense a question about to emerge and would issue his first shot by calling out, "What's that your're eating?" Some would scratch their heads and in confusion walk away. Others might look behind to see who he was talking to, or if there was someone behind them eating something. A few would ignore the comment as misdirected and present their questions anyway as though nothing had been said to them.

On this occasion, a particularly clever villager rose to the challenge, "I don't know. Tell me. What is it I'm eating?"

"You're eating excrement!"

The villager gave a look of surprise, then puzzlement. There was nothing there of course. He wasn't really eating anything. At least nothing we would think of as food was passing over his lips. This was a matter of two tigers in a cave, testing each other's guile.

"What do you mean I'm eating excrement?"

"Don't ask me what I mean, I'm already telling you, you're eating excrement!"

"Would it be better if I had some soup?" the villager responded, making light of it.

You see, the villager was mocking, but also challenging the master. Not unlike the hunter trying to coax the tiger out of his lair.

"Does the word excrement confuse you? It's shit. Don't step in it, and don't eat it, and don't keep it floating around in your head. And don't try to change it into soup with words!"

"Do you think everyone else eats it?"

"I see only you before me. You're eating excrement!"

Unable to catch the meaning or the intent, and feeling he was perfectly normal in all respects, the villager could only say in his defense, "There are worse things to eat aren't there? If everyone else is doing it, it shouldn't be a problem."

"Ah yes, everyone else! Isn't that really who we hope to be when you think of it? Do and be like them? Eat the same as them? I'm not talking to everyone else. Like everyone else, you come to me seeking wisdom," replied the old master, adding "Listen carefully, this is for your ears only, not everyone else's. Forget about them. YOU'RE EATING SHIT!"

As he said this, he looked in anticipation to the villager, as though expecting something profound to happen. An explosion perhaps. Maybe the top of a head popping off. Perhaps even a trickle down a pant leg.

Getting no response, he began to giggle, then to laugh outright. He shook his head to whip the drip from his nose.

The villager reacted, "I don't understand why you're calling what's in here (tapping the side of his head for good effect) excrement. How would you know if you haven't tried it."

The old man's eyes rolled heavenward, "I can see clearly what it is, look carefully, focus, you'll see it for what it is too."

The villager answered defensively, "I don't see it, I don't smell it. And if you ask me right now, I can honestly say I don't taste it, or that it actually tastes just fine. Can you tell me why that is?"

"See!!!"

"What???"

"There's the proof! You're eating crap! And you're reveling in it!"

"Just tell me why you keep saying I'm eating crap."

"Beats me, I figure you don't know better, so I'm trying to help. But it's all over you, inside and outside, and in your heart and muddling your thoughts. Look there! It's even on the tip of your tongue! Hurry, wipe it off!"

"Why do you think you can figure that out and I can't? Maybe you're too self important for your own damn good."

"I don't know why I can and you can't. That doesn't concern me. Your question beats me like a stick against the skin of a living drum sitting before you. A sound emerges from the vibration, you don't like what you hear or what the sound represents. To me, it's just a sound, no sweat off my back! No different than a dog barking, except you take it so personally. Why? You're questioning me about eating crap, and my only answer can be, you're eating crap! You are because you are! You're putting excrement in your mouth. And then you're swallowing it. It's flowing around inside you, drowning your spirit and settling in your center for thinking. What a putrid smell! Stop spewing it at me!"

Shocked and offended, the villager demanded, "Why does my being like every other normal person so offend you?"

"You came here! You're asking me! I'm answering. You're the drummer, I'm the sound. You're the image, I'm the emptiness in the mirror."

Trying to one up the master, the villager thought for a moment then spoke. "Did you know it comes in flavors?"

Of course at this point, old Jou was laughing so hard, his teapot fell to the walkway.

"I don't doubt it comes in flavors. That's still crap you're eating. Crap cherry, crap vanilla, crap apple, all crap!"

The villager thought he had him. "You know, since there's so much demand, and everyone seems to be eating it, I could start selling it."

"Some do. Not me. That's crap on top of excrement. You've outdone yourself. Why do you even tell me? You don't need my approval, or disapproval. Go ahead and sell it. Be wealthy, accumulate more crap, show it off, wear it, think it, speak it. Become it if you will. There's only one choice you have, be crap, or flush the toilet. Dirty water, clean water, look closely, you'll figure it out soon enough."

"I'm curious. Does everybody eat crap like I do?"

"That stuff you're putting into your mouth, chewing, and swallowing. Even your question. That's horse shit. Still crap in the end!"

"Is there anything that's not?"

"Me!" (For a moment, Old Jou wiped the smile from his face, staring sternly as though emphasizing something important had just been said.)

Trying to turn it around, the villager replied, "Oh, so now you think you're hot shit!"

"No, I am who I am. You can think of it as hot shit, or sticky shit, or dog shit. That's your thought to carry."

He horse chuckled through his nose and half laugh snorted.

"Wake up! See for yourself. Better to stop eating the crap first. It fogs your vision, clouds your thoughts, undermines your senses and muddles your spirit. On top of that, it's grimy as hell and stinks to high heaven."

"Looking at you, old master, I don't see anything so different or so special."

"That's a start!"

"You're speaking riddles!"

"That's crap!"

"What kind of wise man are you, you're wasting my time."

"Thank you. May I leave?"

"Not until you tell me what your problem is," said the villager.

The elder looked at the villager as though he were a simpleton. Then like a bolt of lightning, his hand reached across the open space separating them and slapped the simpleton's head. "You're eating shit you imbecile! Stop eating shit and see what happens!"

The perplexed look on the face of the simpleton drew a burst of laughter from the elder.

It almost happened for the simpleton, but not quite.

The gift of enlightenment is a gift that comes at dear cost. The you whom you value so highly must leave stage center! A sacrifice few are prepared to make, even as truth calls out your bluff.

The moment having passed, the opportunity gone, the master, laughing with even more gusto, stood, turned away, and set off.

"Wait, don't go, I offended you, I apologize, come back, we need you!"

"Sorry, I won't be part of your diet. It's simply too rich for my taste" the elder replied, and laughed even more heartily.

"Will you come again?"

"Never!" he walked, continuing his laughter, now even further away from the shit eater.

After some some distance, the old man turned, "Perhaps someday you'll reach your gluttonous full, and then you'll have no choice but to let it go. Stick your finger down your throat and puke it out. With luck, you'll understand, and perhaps even have a laugh with me."

SILENCE

Then, laughing back in ridicule (perhaps hoping to make a final fatal thrust at the wily old tiger), the villager called out, "I think you're full of shit too!"

Hysterical laughter faded in the distance, with the old man's final words, "I suppose I deserved that."

So there you have it. The others who witnessed alongside me mumbled among themselves. I overheard one of them say, "I know I just saw something profound, but I have no idea what the hell it was."

It was another time, and in the aftermath, I thought about it often. Some years after I had witnessed the exchange, I had the good fortune to encounter Master Jou in yet another town center. He recognized me immediately and gave his usual warm nod of greeting, along with a welcoming smile. By this time, several villagers had already gathered, already impatient for his attention and counsel.

He stared expectantly, then unexpectedly turned toward me, as though directing all of their eyes to see what would happen.

A smile lit slowly across my face, I turned, and with a slow odoriferous pppffffffftttt emerging from my rear in the general direction of Laughing Jou, I walked away from my questions forever!

I could hear his laughter echoing off the walls for quite some time.

Challenges

The price of notoriety in the martial arts is the "Challenge." Once you're established as a prominent competitor, fighter, or instructor, it's only a matter of time before you become a stepping stone in someone else's search for recognition. It's dog eat dog, big eat small, code of the west, only the strong survive, call it what you will. In the end, the burden of talent is having to prove it against all comers. As with boxers, there is ultimately only one possible final outcome. That is, to relinquish the prize, seldom willingly, through defeat. Though recent years have produced several middle aged champions, the harsh reality remains that as you age, your physical and mental processes gradually deteriorate. In the end, you succumb. Only the shadow of achievement remains. Unless...perhaps...you have mastered your art beyond the physical.

"You only have to do two things to beat me. Knock me down, and keep me down!" Sensei said this hundreds of times and I knew the words well. "If you can knock me down and keep me down, I will take my belt off, and give it to you. I'll call you Master!"

He made it clear from our first meeting. If ever I felt superior to him as a martial artist, the door was open for me to take his belt, if I could. I was one of the knowing few. He and I had worked together. I was permitted to feel his power first hand. How to describe the many occasions when I would throw a kick or a punch and suddenly, not knowing how, found myself floating in the air, face to ceiling, back to the floor, Sensei's elbow in my rib cage, fingers in my eyes, then hitting the floor while his elbow dug deep into my chest pinning me helplessly to the ground. Always, at the last instant, the technique relaxed, as I flirted with unconsciousness.

Until working with Sensei, my "fight" consisted of sending single techniques through openings in opponents' defenses, blocking and parrying, avoiding, dodging, trapping, tripping, sweeping, throwing and disabling, laid out like pearls on a string. This changed when I met Sensei. When he executed, everything happened at once. Frankly, it took me years of exposure before I could even begin to "see" the things he was doing.

Having experienced the complexities of his responses, I was puzzled that when working with other students, his response to attacks would be on a more basic level. I observed differences in the way he taught different students. Our group worked out as a class, and sometimes as individuals. He would move about, and during interfaces with each of us, impart discrete units of knowledge which became cornerstones for each student's own foundation to fighting.

"The teacher must measure the student. A good parent does not put a loaded gun into the hand of an infant. The teacher must know the mind, the spirit and heart of the student, lest by accident he provide weapons the student does not have the maturity to handle." With each student, he tailored a course appropriate for that student to follow.

There were some elementary reasons for Sensei's hesitancy to teach everything to everyone. For one thing, his store of knowledge was immense. During my time with Sensei, whenever I was exposed to a new technique, he would insist I leave the workout area, record the technique, then return. I would go to the side and try to describe the new technique verbally into a recorder, to be transcribed when I returned home. Now, I have volumes of transcripts, and within them, I can't think of any lessons being repeated.

Others, were not so fortunate as I. There were some who worked with him for years, and learned little more than how to throw punches and kicks. Sensei would explain, "I taught them what they asked to learn. They wanted fight...fight...fight, speed and power, speed and power! I would have given them anything, but that is what they asked for, and, in their own way, they were telling me what they could be responsible for." Undoubtedly, Sensei's judgment in this area was impeccable, for inevitably, these types would receive their black belts then proclaim soon after that they had mastered the art, and could defeat even Sensei in open competition.

Sensei fully understood human nature, and always kept something in reserve.

Perhaps they were foolish, perhaps innocently naive, but broadcasting such reckless comments about a man so committed to honor and the martial way was playing with fire.

In public, Sensei wore a red sash. "I never used to wear a red sash, but I saw what everyone else was teaching, and they would wear their black belts, their first degrees, their second degrees, and they said they could do this and that, and they could do kata and they could break bricks and boards, but when I watch them move, there is nothing of substance. Meeting me, they would ask what style I had studied. Style!!! It is just a word. Like tree! Horse! Apple! Someone who truly understands the martial arts, never asks questions about style. He already knows there is only one style, and that style is you and what is inside you! I don't pretend to be the best. Maybe I am, maybe I'm not. I don't know the answer to that, and I really don't care to know. I do know that I'm pretty good, and that all somebody has to do to beat me is knock me down and keep me down. To make it worth their while, a long time ago, that's why I put on a red sash, and created my own "Style." I really didn't want to do it, but I guess I had to do it because whenever people would ask me what my style was, I felt I had to give them a good answer. Something they could relate to. So, my style is Wai Yu Fu. If you mess with me, you're bound to hear, "Why, you fool?"

Sensei would laugh uncontrollably when he said this.

Quite honestly, I never did figure whether this explanation was true, and if that was really how he evolved the name of his style. Just possibly, the only reason he wore the red belt was so those around him would know that he viewed his skills as being on a plane above theirs, and as such, warranted a special level of recognition. I knew him well enough to know the recognition meant nothing, and the belt was of no meaningful consequence. What he was saying to the world was "You are invited to learn from me about the heart of the martial arts. To make it worth your while, I offer two things, my friendship to you who come in peace, or my red sash, mark of a master, to those of you who come to challenge." Inevitably, those who came as challengers left with nothing.

It was a beautiful autumn day, and we had been working techniques at Sensei's camp in the woods. I was off on my own when the trail of dust rising on the driveway told me a car was fast approaching. The driver pulled up beside the manufactured home where Sensei and his family resided. The driver stepped out, too hurried to shut the car door, and went to Sensei's oldest son, Jason, also a student.

"Are you the Master?"

"No, you're looking for my Dad, he's over there," Jason replied, as though he had gone through this same routine many times in the past. With a flick of his head, Jason motioned that I follow him, and we both trailed behind the impetuous stranger, as he fast approached Sensei.

What always amazed me about these guys was their total lack of creativity in challenging someone to a fight. I mean, even those of us who aren't martial artists have seen enough Kung Fu movies to know that you don't walk up to a master, or someone you think may be a master, or even someone you think may not be a master, but you're not sure, and then demean him to his face. It doesn't take a mental giant to appreciate that if the guy's for real, then what you're doing is tantamount to asking for a tattoo across the front of your face. "Idiot!" I thought.

Well, as this stranger closed on Sensei, it was clear he stood well over six feet tall, and looked to weigh more than 225 pounds. He was heavily muscled, and projected an air of confidence, strength, and determination. If I were to mold a quintessential "image" of challengers, he might even fit the bill.

"Are you the Master?", he barked, looking down at Sensei.

Jason silently mimicked the words he had heard so many times before.

"What can I do for you sir?", responded Sensei, already knowing the response would be "I've heard that you're a master and that you're supposed to be a great fighter, but I know that I can beat you." It always eventually got down to the bottom line. "Sir, all you have to do be the master is knock me down, and after you knock me down, keep me down. That's it!" At this point, Sensei would be silent, expecting everything.

For me, this first time was a study in contrasts. The challenger wore his martial arts ability like a neon sign, flashing it in every direction, as though it were a badge of power with which he could intimidate, cajole, dominate or suppress whoever or whatever might cross his path. Sensei stood casually in what to all but the most experienced eye was little more than a relaxed standing position. He did not have to "wear his fight" to project skill.

"Well, I'm waiting," Sensei delivered his usual words of encouragement to the challenger, who then assumed a preferred fighting stance. To Sensei's eye, this guaranteed any move the challenger made from that point would be projected beforehand in time to react with an appropriate counter. Instantly, the side of the challenger's left foot was rocketing towards Sensei's head. It appeared to be a certain hit, but for the fact when the foot arrived at the space where Sensei's head had been, there was nothing. Sensei was already on the ground, snaking his feet around the challenger's supporting leg, slamming him down, face forward, to the ground. There was a loud thud as the man's weight flattened like a bag of flour onto the woodland floor.

When he rose to his feet, I could see his nose and his mouth were bloodied, and as though reading lines from a script, Jason whispered into my ear, "You were lucky that time...there's no way in hell you're going to do that again" predicting the challenger's words as he again squared off against Sensei.

Sensei approached him, stopping a respectful distance from his front and replied, "Sir, now don't get me wrong, because I'm not trying to put you down. With the way you fight, I could do anything I want to you, and there's not a thing you could do to stop me."

True or not, this was waving the red flag in front of a wounded bull. There was a scream, as the challenger exploded forth with multiple hand and foot techniques. Without changing positions, Sensei melted away from the several incoming attacks. The only counter visible to myself and Jason was a lightning punch to the challenger's sternum as Sensei stepped inside the attack.

Within martial arts circles, there is much chatter and rumor about what is called the "one inch punch." Depending on the legend, the story, or the account, the one inch punch is theoretically executed from a distance of approximately one inch from the target, but because of the dynamics, the true "one inch punch" is supposed to have the full impact and power of a punch thrown from a maximum power position.

Well, whether or not this was the one inch punch, I can't say. To me, it looked as though Sensei had merely touched the challenger with a close in movement. There was a sound like an awl splitting a wooden log, and the challenger hurtled backwards through space landing on the ground writhing in pain.

Sensei approached and said, "Well friend, you're down again!" At which point the challenger got up to execute another attack, using his remaining energy. A last effort to recover his honor. There was a second punch, and I knew it was over as the challenger flipped over backwards, shoulders dipping to the ground, feet lifting skyward.

He would not get up again. Lying there in pain, his last conscious words were "You win!" which Jason, standing to my front, had already begun to parrot as the challenger whispered them a second time, through teeth gritted in pain.

From the background, Sensei's whispered words floated by on the breeze, "Why, you fool?"

Three Times Around the Circle

Lau Wei had come to the Southern Highlands by way of the Chinese Nationalist Army. As a loyal member of the Gwomingdang, he had spent the twenty prime years of his life warring. When their cause had become corrupt, and defeat certain, the Gwomingdang retreated to Taiwan. He parted from them, heading South, choosing his own future.

He was a peasant. At birth, he passed from the midwife's hands onto the earthen floor and was bound to the earth ever since. His father was a peasant, as was his mother, his aunts, uncles, grandparents, and on before. For hundreds of years, his family worked the land, and, after generations of marriage among neighbors most of the villagers came to acquire the family name "Wei," and so it was. Were it not for war, he would have remained in the village of Wei, and by now would have been an honored elder. Had nature's course held true, he would have had many children, and even more grandchildren, which he would have prepared carefully for their own lives in the village Wei.

But the years of war changed that. First was the anarchy, stirred by the warlords; then the nationalist struggle; and then the occupation by the Japanese; and finally, the revolution. When all was over, the village of Wei had disappeared. The people, his people, were gone.

So, having nothing to return to, he chose to go South.

Only those closest to him knew that he had spent his youth in the Temple of Hwang Lung. As was the case in many pre-revolution villages, youths with promise were hand selected from among the many to learn the skills of the ancestors. The chosen ones eventually became the village leaders, as well as the healers, teachers, priests, and protectors.

In line with temple custom, the flat bottom of novice Wei's right foot was tattooed with a dragon, its fiery breath pointed frontward. The left bore a raised hand. These were the traditional marks of one charged to suppress evil. He was a protector. The brands had been placed in those places so only the holder need know of their existence, and their significance.

Spending his later years in the South, he worked the land and kept to himself. Except for chosen students, no one knew his secret, that he was the twenty first master in the line from Southern Mountain. Because he was a healer, and a renowned thinker, the peasants venerated him, though they seldom lured him away from the land he worked and loved.

Eventually, other scions of the Guomingdang also turned South, especially when the Cultural Revolution of the North marked a dramatic end to their reign of influence. But these men journeyed South for reasons other than peace. The peasants of the South proved no match for the displaced warlords. In just a few short years, the harvest changed from rice to opium. The dust roads, meant to carry oxen, now bore the crisp tire marks of western limousines, inevitably preceded and followed by the staccato tracking of armored vehicles. The peasants, who had never before experienced poverty, were now desperately poor. Their families had become weak, and households with eligible daughters were few.

The southern village of Chu Nan lay in a most fertile but inaccessible valley, protected by a limestone gorge, through which only one man and a cart could safely pass together. The warlords coveted the fertile valley for its rich soil, and for its natural defenses, but could not gain influence with its traditional elders, many of whom over time had become disciples of Lau Wei.

It was clear. The interests of the warlords required they solve the problem of Lau Wei. Killing him would be inappropriate. But surely, humiliating him would weaken his influence among the leaders, and the ambitious youth, tipping the scales to the interests of the warlords, and allowing the desired foothold into the valley. They knew once they gained entry to the protected valley, they could never be forced to leave, by insiders, or by outsiders.

They searched long and far for a warrior certain to defeat the old man.

After they found him, this is what came to pass.

It was mid morning of the seventeenth day of the harvest month. Change was in the morning air, and steam bellowed from the sweated students who attacked the blindfolded Wei. Though 72 years old, when Wei demonstrated "fighting blind," his speed and power were that of a man much younger.

On that day, a stranger entered the camp.

Finishing the drill, Wei removed his blindfold, announcing that he would journey to the market for two days in search of buyers for his crop, but before he could finish his thought, he turned slowly and sighted the one whom he already knew had come with malicious intent.

"Welcome stranger. How may I serve you?"

"If you are Wei. I have come to test you."

In the distance, the old man saw the cool mist lift slightly from Cat Lake. Laughing children played to his rear, and in the far distance, a dog barked.

Facing the stranger, he answered, "For what purpose shall I submit to your test?"

Unyielding, the challenger spoke, "If you defeat me, you will have great honor."

The old man laughed, shaking his head. A snake darted in the grass at his feet. "No disrespect meant. Honor I have. It is peace which my weary bones seek."

"That is not an acceptable response, old man!"

"Then fight my students!" the old man, clearly annoyed, added. "Don't disturb me today, I am headed to market."

Ju Ming, a young peasant, stepped between them and, facing the stranger, warned "We are peaceful people here. You are not welcome...," but before he could finish, he was down and unconscious.

The old man motioned for others to assist, trembling and angry that his failure to act promptly had allowed an innocent to be injured.

Eyeing the stranger, his brows arched upward as he hissed, "You refuse from a cursed womb. In my time I have dispatched countless mongrel dogs of your ilk to their karmic reward. You defile the very earth on which you stand, and your presence here offends my land and threatens to curse my harvest."

The old man had already kicked dirt onto the stranger, but when he punctuated his tirade by spitting at the stranger, everyone, including the stranger, was shocked. All stood silent. The wind tossed the husky caps of rice. From within his jacket, the stranger whipped out a short sword, and in one fluid motion, attempted to slice the old man from left clavicle to right hip. But the old man nimbly avoided the strike, heckling that, "You come for honor, but slash at an unarmed old man, intending to kill the innocent. Did not your teacher explain righteous conduct to you?"

"I am a man of honor," responded the challenger, defensively, as he threw down the blade and tossed off his jacket. He stood before the old man like a tiger, timing the movement of a grazing doe, patiently tempering its appetite for the certain kill. "You have your challenge, neither of us will leave until you recognize it!"

"What I recognize is that another worm has surfaced from the excrement to announce it has come to defeat me. But the worm knows nothing about who I am, or what I can do. I will grant you this. I now challenge you! If you defeat my challenge, then I will acknowledge that you are my master."

The old man turned to his students, "You have all heard this. Will you bear witness?" Instantly, they swore to witness what was to follow. That satisfied the stranger, whose taut upper torso glistened in the warming sun.

The challenger issued forth, "Then throw your challenge old man!"

Walking to a clearing, the old man knelt on the ground and with his finger, scribed a circle in the soft black earth. Laughing, the young man bellowed, "Surely, that cannot be our arena. There is barely room for me to stand within the circle."

"True, but that is my challenge. Once you accept, you will enter the circle, and try to stay within. I will walk three times around it. If you are able to resist my powers, and I warn you now, that they are far greater than you might imagine, then I will declare you victor and leave the valley forever. If you fail, and if you are a man who values honor, you will leave as you came. There will be no disgrace. I will not humiliate you."

The challenger's steel hard body attested to a lifetime of physical discipline. He walked to the circle, eyed the old man and the students, looked again at the circle, and, confident that he could defend the circle against all present, stepped within, then, looking at the old man, announced, "I accept."

The old man knelt before the stranger, chanting sutras in the classical dialect, which no one present could understand. A student mumbled that "The old man must be calling upon the spirits for power." Hearing this, the challenger studied the old man closely, thinking only how well the old coot concealed his fear over what was, in the challenger's own mind, an inevitable outcome.

"I assume that after you've lost, old man, that my colleagues can use your land to introduce the new crop?"

The old man stood, continued his chant, and circled the challenger.

Beads of perspiration began to trail down the stranger's forehead. Was he feeling unsteady, or was it his imagination? The late morning sun glowed warm beating against his flesh. He eyed his jacket, sitting useless in the distance. He asked for someone to pass it to him. No one moved.

He was not intending to be anyone's fool. "You'll have to do better than this old man. Did you say you had daughters to throw in with the bargain?"

The old man fell flat to the ground. In his mind's eye was the image of a midwife, minding an infant on an earthen floor. A disciple called out, "See how he draws strength from the earth, stranger!"

Lau Wei, again rose, and stood tall, his face void of expression, empty of emotion. He circled the stranger a second time, performing the five animals breathing form. The sound of his breath was one with the wind tossing against the soon to be harvested rice, one with the barking dog, and one with the harmony of the land.

The challenger stood hypnotized, recognizing from his movement that the old man was indeed a great master. When the old man completed the second circuit, the challenger jolted back to reality, then called out, "You are a cobra, old man, but putting me to sleep has not caused me to leave the circle."

The old man faced the stranger, "Think sir, inside, how do you feel?" For an instant, the challenger's concentration broke, and his consciousness flashed that the sun had scarcely moved in the sky, but his skin was burning, as were his innards. It seemed he had been standing there all afternoon, but it had been mere moments. No sooner had the thought surfaced, then his discipline purged any more of it from further distracting him. He looked again, now regretfully, at his jacket sitting uselessly out of reach.

The old man walked close to the circle, and stood defiantly before the stranger. "You have already failed the challenge, but lack the insight to recognize it. Someday, you will appreciate my challenge was an act of mercy to you and was all I could do to spare your life. Hopefully, you will be a better man for it." As he finished the words, his body exploded toward the stranger, stopping just short of the circle. The stranger, reacting only on instinct, had struck out at the old man with such ferocity that the witnesses felt uncertain that the old man would prevail. Fortunately, the challenger's discipline held him in rein long enough for his consciousness to recognize the old man's ploy, and to stop himself from exiting the circle. He broke off the response.

"Very good," responded the young man, still in control, even though his heart was pumping wildly. "First you hypnotize me, then you shock me. What tricks will follow next?"

"These are not tricks," Wei responded, "It was important for the witnesses to see who you were, and the level of your skill, we agreed that there should be witnesses. All that remains for me to do is to walk the circle one more time. I assure you that when I have completed my third trip around the circle, it will be empty."

The thumping cadence which was the old man's voice gripped the challenger's spine. It was not a natural sound coming from the throat of a man. Sweating in the mid-day sun, the stranger felt a snake coiling within his spine, gripping ever so tightly. For an instant, he imagined he had been cast helplessly into the world of the dead, forever detached from the prospect of proper burial with his own ancestors.

The old man approached, smiling, and asked "Do you wish words before you leave?"

The stranger's defiant but questioning stare answered for itself.

The old man turned about, calling his students to come close. "It is already into the afternoon heat, and I have delayed my trip to the market long enough. I will be going for two days, and will return on the third. There will be no class during the interim. You should all take the time to make preparations for your own harvests. I will return on the twentieth day of harvest month, and at mid-morning, class will commence with my walking the circle for the final time. I ask that all of you who stand as witnesses remain to monitor our friend and be here to confirm the final outcome of the challenge."

With that, the old man left for his journey to market. The stranger could manage only silence.

There was great merriment in the valley when Wei returned to perform his final course around the circle. By then, word had spread afar to the outer reaches of the valley, and all who heard, came to "witness" the outcome. The stranger, of course, was gone. In the end, he proved true to his word, a man of honor.

After several more harvests, Wei, too was gone. The time to rejoin his ancestors had come.

The peasants in the valley carried his ashes to the valley's entrance, where they were enshrined with great ceremony.

The characters carved onto the monument read "Lau Wei, teacher, protector, man of peace." Above the characters, etched into the limestone, was a white Buddha, sitting in lotus. Looking closely, one could barely discern what appeared to be the image or outline of a dragon on the sole of its right foot. The left hand of the statue was raised, palm outward, in what all who saw recognized to be the classic position for suppressing evil.

To this day, the village remains intact, and the valley at peace.

Talgos

The dojo door swung wide as the dark eyed stranger entered. With him was a companion, who, mirroring the attitude, expression, and posture of the dark eyed one, proclaimed to all he was a trusted student and disciple. The dark eyed one was Talgos, and his reputation fell like a shadow before him. I knew of rumors about a martial artist who came to the mainland from Hawaii and had singlehandedly shut down schools of instructors who failed to give him allegiance. Such strong arm tactics were rare in the martial arts, but, as does oppression in all forms, they continued to survive, even in our supposedly enlightened and more civilized era.

Talgos was a renegade proponent of Kajukenbo, a powerful hybrid style employing moves and techniques from Karate, Judo, and Chinese boxing, and he purported to be a master of Kung Fu.

A curtain of silence fell as he stalked into the room. He had invested years developing a mixture of body language and countenance which tugged hard at that loop of human consciousness tied directly to the core of our being, wherein lie the base animal fears. No doubt, he liked to stare at goats. He was dangerous, and as he passed stillness and anticipation followed. There were clearly no limits to his audacity or what he would do to accomplish his objectives. Before he uttered a word, all knew that whoever crossed him would risk paying a terrible price.

I was visiting the school that particular evening. A friend, who was a student in the class, knew of my long time interest in the arts and invited me to the class to give my impressions about his Sensei. I met the instructor before class. His name was Blake Foley, and he presented as a gentlemanly thirty five year old with a slightly receding hairline. He was a daytime office worker, who managed to attain a Black Belt while once stationed with the Army on Okinawa.

"I am a strict traditionalist. My students practice under the same code that I learned, under the same rigorous conditions."

He tried to impress me with his Bushido, but I could see as he moved during the early part of the class his stances were flawed, his balance poor, and his technique wanting. That's not a judgment. Many Black Belts are like that. It often takes decades for the art to refine within a person. He weighed approximately one hundred sixty pounds, and stood to the level of my eyes, approximately five foot eight inches tall. "He's terrific," my friend had told me, and with the innocence of the unknowing, believed all this gentleman had to say regarding the martial arts.

Talgos, entering, focused immediately on Blake. Like an eagle homing on its prey the dark-eyed predator angled directly toward the front of the room.

He landed before Blake and turned to the class, "I am a master of Kung Fu. I am three times World Champion Full Contact Karate Fighting, and am in the Martial Arts Hall of Fame. I have worked with Bruce Lee, and with other masters. I am a ninth level Black Belt in Chinese Kung Fu, and a tenth dan in the Filipino stick fighting arts."

I was startled, perhaps even stunned. Rarely had I witnessed such an arrogant display of such unmitigated lies. Sadly, it had become more common. Liars spinning their fabrications have all seemed to learn that forgoing restraint made everything all the more credible. Certainly all present recognized he had grossly distorted the truth, conjuring up his own reality.

Yet, all remained silent, some even impressed by his audacity. Until that moment, I has no idea what brought him to our midst. Originally, I thought he was an invited guest, as was I. Now, I feared to be witnessing a power play.

Talgos turned to Blake, "Who is your instructor?" Blake murmured some barely audible response to Talgos.

"How long have your studied? What right do you have to be teaching Kung Fu here? Where are your credentials? Anyone who teaches Kung Fu answers to me. Did I say you could teach Kung Fu?"

He turned to the class, "I am a master, and it is my right to ensure the true heart of the martial arts is preserved and not watered down as it is being done here. I revoke this man's license to teach. From this moment, I am your teacher, and he is not. He'll do as I say, and you will learn what I teach."

I stood witnessing this monster usurping the class of a lessor skilled martial artist. I knew his representations were false. Though I had heard his technique was powerful and his abilities genuine, it was certain he was never a champion and had never been nominated or elected to any Hall of Fame. He was lying about that too, but no one had the courage to call his bluff, including myself.

If one freezes in the presence of such dark forces, where is the value in the years of training. The thought raced circles around my head until I observed that Blake had finally regained his composure and declared to Talgos, "Sir, I am prepared to tell you who I am, and who my teacher is but first, I'd like to know who you are, who taught you, where you are from, and why you are here." It was a poor effort to play turnabout with Talgos, and pushed him to flashpoint. Like an animal possessed, Talgos leaped at Blake, right hand grabbing Blake's neck, lifting him off the ground and pinning him to the wall. I scarcely believed what my eyes told me. Talgos, who at first appeared to be about the same size and weight as Blake, suddenly had grown two feet taller, and fifty to sixty pounds heavier. The physical transformation confounded me. Did it really happen, or was I being victimized by my own hysteria?

Blake shook with terror, dangling by the neck from the wall. The students of the class stood motionless, perhaps hoping some miracle would undo all that was unfolding before them. The young ones were staring down at the floor, the adults, at Blake, in horror. I glanced at my friend and saw the glimmer of pained tears lining his cheeks. "Can't somebody do something," he whispered.

With experience, a martial artist develops a special "eye" that enables him to see the true skill of an opponent before the first blow is ever thrown. I saw that Talgos had generated tremendous power in a move toward Blake that was virtually flawless. I knew that I could not do likewise, and though I had never seen this man fight, was already sure his skill could top mine.

"It's not your problem," I thought. "Leave before something ugly happens here, and you get involved in something that's not your business." My years of training had give me a spectrum of built in alarms, all of which were ringing wildly at this point. Could I leave with the situation as it now stood? Could I walk out and abandon Foley, this stranger instructor for whom I now felt close kinship and concern? If I did, how long would it before the problem followed me to some other place?

As though reading my thoughts, Talgos turned and focused his burning gaze onto my eyes, "Do you have anything to say?"

Bitter day! The chalice had fallen into my lap before I could safely rationalize leaving. My escape now blocked by ill fate. I held the gaze and carefully circled the dojo, walking to the headspace, when, as I approached, Talgos released the hold on Blake's neck, letting him drop to the ground gasping for air. As I closed, I vowed that whatever happened, Talgos would pay a price for targeting me. I knew that I could not exercise restraint against a force this powerful. My only hope would be to bar no holds, attack all targets, and seek to maim, kill, and destroy. By the time I stood before him, approximately four feet to his front, I was committed. I began, "It seems to me you're trespassing here. Quite obviously, whatever welcome you had when you came through the door has been exhausted. Clearly, the time has come for you and your friend to leave."

Talgos barked, "Are you telling me to leave? Do you intend to back up those words? Are you ready to pay the price?"

I held his stare with my eyes. It was like staring into a deep well. Though he appeared still and at ease, I knew instinctively that any moment, he could explode at me. I would be tested merely to react before going down. With an air of supreme, deliberate confidence, I turned to my friend, now backed against the far wall, "John, this gentleman has entered the school uninvited, has offended its ideals, and has refused to leave when asked. He has already committed an act of violence. Phone the police. We will need their assistance in resolving this criminal intrusion."

Talgos was notably impressed I had the wherewithal and discipline to move my gaze from his, completely turning my sight from his direction, without transmitting fear or uncertainty through the language of my body. Even with experienced attackers, four feet separation could just as well be a canyon. This was a skill I had mastered through years of internal discipline and practice of bodily movements. As my eyes returned to him, John left the floor to make the call. Talgos was beginning to lose control. Staring, I pointed at the nearest student and half jokingly instructed that she better "run outside and jot down the license number of the vehicle our visitors came in, just in case (forcing a laugh) after my demise, the police needed leads on the identity of my assailant." Behind the left shoulder of Talgos, I could see his associate becoming nervous, and his eyes darted back and forth between me and the front door. A siren sounded in the distance as Blake got off the floor and firmly stood his ground, sporting a new found aura of confidence. Now it was two against two.

Talgos edged closer towards where I stood. I expected an attack at any instant, and in my mind, had already exercised strikes to his eyes and vitals as he made his move. Having a plan always came first. There would be no holding back. "What do you intend to do now, tough guy," he snarled at me.

Recovering my distance, I answered, "The way I see it, Sifu Talgos, is that one of four things will happen before we're finished.

"First, I may defeat you in a fight. I should warn that if you make a move on me, I'll do whatever I have to do to end the encounter. If I beat you, it will only be after you have executed the first strike on me, as it is not in my art to ever attack without provocation. Undoubtedly, if I am able to overcome your technique you will sustain serious injury, as my focus will be to destroy you. On top of that, when the police arrive, we will no doubt press charges against you and your colleague as trespassers and for creating a disturbance on the premises.

"Second, and I probably should allow this is the more likely outcome, you will execute a surprise move similar to what you did earlier, and establish a sequence which will ultimately end in my defeat, but hopefully not my demise. Again, I must warn you that I will do whatever I have to do to slow, distract, weaken, destroy, resist or hinder your attack. Suffice it to say that if you make a move on me, I expect to make you pay a dear price that will permanently linger in your memory. I warn you. I have the requisite skills. Furthermore, if I lose after you attack me, you will have even more explaining to do to the police than with the previous outcome. Not to belabor the point, but I should point out I have a high paying job, and a house full of kids, all of whom rely upon me for their sustenance. If I am victimized by your criminal brutality, I intend not only to press charges, but also to pursue you for those expenses and damages which I would be entitled to by law.

"The third possibility is we will not fight, and you will continue to exercise your mental dynamics and power plays with me until the police do arrive, again, at which time we will ask they remove you from the premises, but only after Blake has had ample opportunity to report your physical assault on his person. It's only natural a restraining order will follow."

"And last?" taunted Talgos.

"Last? The last option would be for you to simply leave, and not ever return to this place, for I assure you, you are no longer welcome here."

"I don't like you," Talgos growled, "We'll meet again...," the threat all too obvious, yet not unexpected. Its what bullies do. Outside in the cool distance, nearing sirens howled. To me it was like the spring breeze blowing after a storm, and came through the open door like a welcome mantra. I knew they probably had nothing to do with what was happening at the moment, but their very sound heightened the tension of the moment, and tilted the politic to my corner. Talgos' companion was visibly agitated. There was silence once again, as when Talgos first entered. Talgos turned to his lackey, "Let's get out of here. We don't need these guys."

After he left, the dojo nervously returned to life. Blake had lost considerable face, and as my friend came toward me, he reached for my hand, shaking it enthusiastically while whispering,"I just want you to know I'm glad you came."

Blake was downcast, and said that he had no future if things like this were still happening in the modern world. I turned to Blake and told him that in all my years experience in the martial arts, I had learned only one hard and fast rule. I was a student. As time went by, I was becoming a better student. Some people were masters, but I was not one of them, and I did not want to be one. Some people called themselves teachers. Again, that was their choice. I was merely a student, and with luck, good fortune, and the grace of God, I would be a damned good student by the time my life drew to a close. I turned to Blake and suggested, "Maybe you should go back to being a student. Of course, you'd still be free to work with your class as a student among students, but your class wouldn't have to reckon with impressions of you and your abilities that quite possibly could prove to be unrealistic."

Blake smiled and responded, "I'm just going to have to think this through."

Author's Note:

The story of Talgos is completely fictional, but reflects actual situations I have witnessed or heard of during my long career. More importantly, Talgos is a metaphor for those challenges sure to come in every person's life when they are confronted by an overwhelmingly powerful antagonist, and have to take a stand. It could be against the school yard bully, an abusive spouse, or a tyrant supervisor. The challenge is always the same. If you don't rise to the oppressor, you become the victim. Underlying the story is the importance of strategy or "politic" in every crisis. My teachers were careful to emphasize every confrontation was steered by a politic, and taught how controlling this politic was precursor to controlling and ultimately overcoming the situation. Go back and revisit the story. See if you can trace how the protagonist finds a successful politic within the otherwise impossible challenge, and ultimately makes the entire stage dance to his tune before he is thru. A darned fine dance indeed!

Thursday Surprise

In boxing, the first sign of a great fighter losing touch is his proclaiming himself to be the peoples' champion. Living in his citadel, surrounded by pumped bodyguards, and suffering from delusions of invincibility, the champion at this point knows no more about being champion of the people, than a roach knows about the Declaration of Independence.

If there's one undeniable benefit to being a master of the martial arts, it's that you have freedom of movement. Sensei could go anywhere he wanted to go, whenever he wanted to. Thoughts about muggings, or late night attacks, or being accosted by street people never barred him from going about his business.

To the contrary. He was popular with the people of the street, and of the night.

Sensei belonged with the people. It's as though he had chosen humility and hardship at some early stage in his life, and by so doing, had forever appended himself to that level of society where earning a living meant struggle and uncertainty. As I recall, each day his efforts barely produced enough for the next day's sustenance. Manual labor had become his destiny.

Destiny or not, he loved physical motion, and even when seen working a jackhammer, or rolling hot asphalt on a smoldering summer roadway, he would be making a study of the physical motions. He experimented with everything, and struck at the opportunity to surprise and challenge those about him.

This story begins when one morning I was awakened by a pounding on my door. "Hey Mac, get out of bed. Let's go to Seattle and see what's happening in Chinatown."

Rolling over, I found it was still dark outside. The soft glow of my night clock outlined five-thirty on the dial. It was Thursday.

When Sensei decided to do something, a timer began ticking impatiently away in his head. When he showed up on your doorstep at dawn, you'd better be ready to go somewhere, and fast.

I tried to coax him into some coffee, and perhaps some breakfast to which he responded, "No Mac. I already ate."

I understood that to mean "Forget the breakfast, get dressed, and let's go."

Within minutes, we were on the road headed North. He was philosophical that morning, setting the tone for the day. Driving up, he bubbled over with recollections about his teachers, and his years at the Temple (he learned his art while spending his youth in Japan, orphaned to a Buddhist

Temple). The way I figured, he was dealing with a heavy sense of nostalgia, and just needed a place to go to, and someone to spend some time with.

I was happy to fit the bill, but I was still famished.

We trekked about Seattle in the early morning, observing people dashing to work. How wondrously detached we were. I was unemployed at that time, and Sensei chose not to work that day. On a different day, in a suit and shaved, I could have been one of those android like creatures, rushing to or fro in tune to some distant refrain. But who am I to be judgmental? Was my plight any better than theirs?

The only time I felt "in control" of my own destiny I was heavy on the skids, out of work, and forced to make strings of decisions about what to do next with my time. Could rushing about as they were be so bad?

As morning wore on, we drifted toward First Avenue and the Public Market. This was always like going to the circus. Thrown together in one spot at one time were the wealthy, the destitute, and the in between. I'm sure the well-to-do came in part to gloat over, or to savor the street people, the potential escorts, the street vendors and the panhandlers, while the people of the street came to market their wares to the wealthy, whatever wares they had to offer. For those with nothing to market, there was always the chance to play some hustle, or to pick someone's pocket.

Framing the human landscape, were the middle class, who would gawk at the wealthy and sidestep the poor, in essence, filling in the spaces necessitated by commerce.

I was sidelined, looking into the window of an antique shop, when, in the reflection, I saw Sensei talking to a group of tattered characters. I overheard "... a worn out old man getting a drink this time of day?" One of them pointed off toward the South side of the market. Sensei nodded his head, showing exaggerated thanks, swinging it up and down in a wild arc. I could see Sensei was doing one of his ingratiating routines, playing dumb and harmless. An act!

I wondered what was up.

Minutes later, we were in the portal to the F&A tavern. Actually, you probably had to be an initiate to even know where the entry to this place was. Sitting on First Avenue, between two vacant store fronts, was a door with a decaled "F&A" on the cracked glass. As we opened the door, our senses were flooded by a warm bubble of moist air from below. When my eyes adjusted to the darkness, I could see a row of steps dropping into the bowels of the Seattle underground. The steps veered hard to the left at bottom.

The sound of voices arguing in the darkness floated upward.

We descended the steps, and with each downward step, the scent of raw humanity grew stronger. I felt I had entered the mouth of some beast, and was slowly glissading down its digestive passageway. How far down would they lead me?

I lost my footing on one of the steps, fell, and in the dim light, saw I had slipped on a load of what appeared to be human excrement. The stench was unbearable. As I got back to my feet, I felt like a complete idiot. Why was I there? I stared questioningly at Sensei, who said nothing.

At the bottom, we turned right and entered a cavernous chamber. I could barely see scattered rows of tables and benches, in no recognizable pattern. We walked forward and after a stop or two I stumbled over the body of a down-at-the-heels, whose torso lay propped against the wall at the edge of the stairs. The undeniable reek of urine poured through my nostrils and flooded my consciousness.

I struggled with my gag reflex to keep things under control. I could see now it was fortunate I hadn't eaten that morning.

"Let's get the hell out of here," I said turning to Sensei, but he was already taking seat at a nearby table, hollering out to some aged leatherskin in the distance to bring over "Two glasses of something cold and wet."

I was getting royally pissed off!

"Mac, how do you like this place?"

"Is that a serious question?" I retorted.

"Don't be so touchy. It's important for you to be here. You've learned about defeat from tournaments, but did you ever wonder what happens to a man whose spirit has been crushed? Look around. For some, it's here. See them first hand. These are the empty shells after human dignity, spirit, and capacity for love have been orphaned. An empty, dark cavern with a vile stench, inhabited by worms and vermin living only for the next indulgence."

He continued, "Think of how you appear right now. To them you could just as well be a camel. You are so different from these creatures. But what makes you so different? Do you deserve a better destiny? Do they deserve worse? Is it fate, karma, cosmic coincidence, God's favor? Now you see it, now you don't. When you leave here, they're gone. Forgotten! These are the mysteries of life which continue unanswered forever. Look. The five men in the corner have already spotted you. I'll bet they're planning to strip you clean. They might even kill you! No one would ever find out if it happened down here."

Sensei continued on, but when he said they might kill me, my panicked gaze riveted on the far end of the pit, where I made out the shapes of moving bodies, where before there had been only shadows. One of them, a bearded man wearing leather bottoms and no shirt, began to drift in my direction. He walked close by, taking notice particularly of me, flashed a look of scorn, then hissed "shit" in contempt. I knew he already hated me, or what he made me out to be. He went on over to the bar, and as I turned my panicked look toward Sensei, I overheard "Who's the faggot with the wetback?"

Though I missed some of his words, Sensei had still been talking, "...and you can't be angry with a scorpion if it stings you when you pick it up. In the same fashion, a shark is a shark. They can't be hated or despised because their conscience is different from ours. For them good is a full stomach. It doesn't matter that some living being has to be shredded to accomplish that. That's the nature of sharks. They don't live by our code. The animals here are like sharks. When hungry, they will strike. Right or wrong is not for us to determine. They have no choice. That, my friend is the ultimate knowledge for a martial artist. That, plus we have the right to react. The right to defend ourselves. It all reduces to eating when you're hungry, sleeping when you need rest, and walking where you please. I'm sure you know, for most, even these simple things sometimes pose great risks, and for that reason you have worked all these years to develop your discipline, your courage, and your skills."

"Good Lord!" I cried out, "The bastards are headed this way!"

Sensei flashed an admonishing glance at my casual use of profanity.

"Stand beside me here, where they can see you better. Let them see your indomitable spirit."

I thought I saw where this was headed. Man was I glad he was with me.

"I might hate this, but I'll tell you, if I have to go down fighting, you're the one I want beside me."

I could say that the five approaching figures looked threatening, but it wasn't that. They were bizarre, like something out of a drunken trance, or a nightmare. One man with leather bottoms and a bare top, the other with cutoff shorts and a sweat shirt, another, skinny as a rail but whose movements exuded feline grace, as he seemed to float toward us. The fourth was twirling a baton like instrument, I couldn't make out what it was. He wore a head band, and looked like he had just walked out of a kung fu movie. The fifth lumbered like a bear. He could have been one for all I knew. When he stepped from shadow into gray light, I saw a face printed over with madness, hate and pain.

I knew Sensei could handle them, and counted myself privileged he stood with me. I wouldn't know what to do if I were alone surrounded by these five, and somehow had to get out.

Sensei, standing beside me, cautioned, "Keep cool, clear your mind, have faith in yourself and your technique. Trust yourself, trust your discipline, trust all those years of commitment and hard work, of doing what you deemed impossible. This is just another step, no different. Tell me, how do you feel?"

With his words, a train of mental images flashed across my mind. I had recollections of walking across hot coals, lying submerged in iced over lakes, climbing out of abandoned wells, and being buried alive. These were all terrifying experiences I had survived, and Sensei had guided me through them safely.

Sensei," I whispered, "I'm ready."

I did feel good. Whole. Complete, even integrated. It was a new experience.

But turning, I found Sensei was gone. I mean, completely gone! He had vanished!

As I searched about frantically, leatherpants came at me, throwing a looping boxer's roundhouse. I ignored the punch and drilled him twice in the forehead with the iron palm, I wasn't taking chances. He was momentarily stunned and blinded when the tail of the dragon smashed against the back of his right knee him slamming to the ground.

Kung Fu came next with his baton, which I ripped from his hand and threw into the far shadows. He threw a side kick with his left leg, but I was already on the ground with cobra, wrapping my feet about his supporting right leg and knee. I rolled onto my shoulder, twisting and snapping. There was a scream of pain, a few choice profanities, and as I rolled to clear, I was distracted by what appeared to be a two foot long rat, staring at me with moon eyes from under the table. Whose nightmare was I in?

I slid beneath the table, to spring up on the other side, where instantly, I was seized from behind by leatherpants, now back on his feet. To my front, a spark in the darkness told me the tip of a knife was headed toward my midsection. Instinctively, I stepped with my right foot across the front of my left, and moved leatherpants from behind me, forward and into the incoming knife. He made no sound, but I knew he was hit. I felt the stream of life pouring from his body.

With both hands, I reached past the falling body to grab the thin man's head. With a corkscrew twist, I drove him headfirst into the ground. His fight was over!

I struggled to remember how many were left. Counting quickly, I knew that three were down, but who remained? My right eye glimpsed a hand about to strike, but I was too late to block, and took a hard head shot, almost knocking me from my feet. As the man in cut offs closed to kick me, I stepped inside instinctively driving the top of my forehead into his nose. At the same time, with a thunderous clap, I slammed my open hands against his ears.

I remembered now. Only one remained. I sighted the "bear" and stood ready to face him square.

He moved toward me, slowly, eying carefully, stopping at attacking distance from my front.

"What brought you here today?"

Stunned speechless, I gaped at him. Was he talking to me? I advanced threateningly but he never moved. I knew to attack was pointless, no way was I going to penetrate his defenses. In fact, unless my eyes deceived, he had taken the dragon stance.

"Circumstances," I answered. "My friend is trying to get rid of me!"

"Was that Sensei I saw you with?"

"Yes," I replied, not believing what I'd just heard. Could he too have studied the arts, yet ended here? In a flash, I realized all things were possible. Good and bad, that nothing stood guaranteed, and that I too might someday find myself at home in one such hopeless pit.

He backed off, turned about, then walked away. As he dissolved into the darkness, a "You'd better get out of here!" reached back to my ears.

Only then, did I begin to feel the aches and to notice the briny taste of blood rolling about in my mouth. I stank, and was filthy. For an instant, I was lost. I was disoriented, and it took me several turns walking aimlessly about the room to find the stairs.

In time, I caught the faint beam of light trickling down from above.

I struggled my way painfully up the stairs. Sensei waited at the top, with a big smile on his face, and a hug.

"I see you survived."

I had no words in response. I was too exhausted to be angry, and was just hoping to make it back to the car. "You're gonna have to drive us home," I said.

"Mac," he said, "I have a present for you."

Looking over to Sensei, I saw him holding a black sash out to me with two extended hands. "Today, you've earned it! You are number five. Four others have received it before you."

"Let's find a place where I can get cleaned up."

With his worn hands, he tied the belt around my waist. I saw my reflection off a storefront window. Passers by wondered what we were up to. I felt like I was on a different planet, thinking about what had just happened. Seeing myself in the glass looking like I had come out of a garbage can, stinking so bad I could scarcely breathe.

We went on down to the water front, where beneath a secluded dock, I stripped down and immersed my aching body into the freezing Puget Sound. The cold water actually soothed my wounds and quieted my pain. I closed my eyes and let go. A soothing minute passed, when a sound from nearby startled me, my eyes sprung open.

As I turned right, I could see that it had again become dark outside, as I once again focused my eyes on the glow. The soft light of my night clock outlined six o'clock on the dial.

My thoughts then ran to my years of study with Sensei in his "ninja hideaway," hidden within the Black Hills outside of Olympia, Washington, and the countless challenges I had faced under his guidance.

Once, he asked if I trusted him, and I answered that I certainly did.

Then he asked, "And if I took you to the middle of a bridge and ordered you to 'Jump!' would you?"

"Yes Sensei, I would!"

"And why would you do that?"

"Because in the years that we've spent together, I've learned to trust you, and that you wouldn't tell me to do something, unless there was a reason. But regardless, you would be there to help me, if I needed you."

Well Sensei didn't believe in giving rank. Our students were white belts, except for four, who of the thousands trained by Sensei, were privileged to wear the color black.

I would have been the fifth, had Sensei not met his tragic end in an ill fated mountain rescue.

When he left, I was alone. The light was turned off.

Aimless years of following the harvests, living hand to mouth, factory labor in San Francisco, laid off, drifting north again to Seattle, in and out of business, up one year, down the next, no time to be happy, but always making time for practicing the art. His art. Don't ask me to explain why! Maybe I ended a past life as a fish on his hook, and it carried over!

I remember now. It seems long ago, but it was only last night. I returned home from work exhausted, as usual, and had a couple drinks, as usual, and as the warm glow enveloped my body, my arms and legs lay tightly against the mattress. My thoughts ran to Sensei, and how nothing in my life seemed so important as wearing his black belt, but it could never be. He left before he had finished. Now, it springs back to mind ... my last thought before sleeping was that he had abandoned me.

Suddenly, awake, my realization is that he had not! The dream was a test! As real as fire! I was his unfinished business, a ship adrift on a turbulent sea. And he had come to make it right. Now I could be whole!

After passing the test, my life found direction of its own. Shortly thereafter, I moved on. I ended in Santa Cruz, it's where I always wanted to live, why not just go there and see what happened? Gradually, success followed, with an end to following the harvests and living hand to mouth. Following my "Thursday Surprise," I visited Seattle only once again. It was years later, on a business trip.

While there, an impulse seized me as my cab drifted slowly past the market place. I turned my head sharply right, and with a mind of their own my eyes locked onto the rubble of an empty lot. There a doorway stood, as though defying gravity. My eyes climbed their way to the cracked window above. I could barely make it out but imprinted on the glass was the letter "F" and the letter "A." I had the cabbie stop for a moment. My reflection stared back at me. I looked younger, and wait; was that the old man waving from behind? Before I could look again, the unit toppled over with a definitive crash of glass shattering all to pieces.

I must remember to compliment Sensei on his sense of humor, and his timing.

Knowing the "F&A." existed brought me full circle. From that day onward, I ate when I was hungry, slept when I was tired, and was free to go wherever I wanted. The chains were broken forever.

The Supermarket

It was a long day. We had traveled up to Vancouver, British Columbia to do a demonstration. As it turned out, the show wasn't until late afternoon so we pretty much had nothing to do the whole day. That, combined with having to sit through the four hour drive to Vancouver had us both a bit edgy when our time came to perform.

Not to worry, it turned out fine, or should I say, as well as could be expected.

When you work with someone as long as I've worked with Mr. Kwan, you know there are days when the technique and execution is perfect, and days when it is not. On this day, it was not. Kwan was troubled, maybe it was the drive, maybe the delay. Who knows? His mind was elsewhere.

Twice, I nearly kicked him doing my attacks. During the knife demo, he missed a block on a straightforward knife thrust. Fortunately, few, if any in the audience noticed the error. As we wrapped up, Kwan said, "Let's get our stuff and hit the road. I'm exhausted." He wanted to leave fast, his discomfort obvious. Kwan had a sense about things, I respected that. If he wanted to leave, then we would.

Within thirty minutes, we had crossed the border and were back in the states. We were both thirsty, and pulled off the interstate to a small town supermarket where we went for soft drinks.

It was Kwan's treat, so while he was in line waiting to pay, I ventured over to the magazine rack.

A headline about an extraterrestrial having impregnated several Kansas farm girls immediately caught my attention, as did the feature about Hollywood pets contracting aids. "How is that possible," I thought, puzzling over the implication inherent in the headline.

As I reached for the tabloid, I was jarred from behind by a passing customer. While my body instinctively positioned for potential trouble, my senses focused on the surrounding environment to sense whether there was a threat.

The air was heavy with a beer-on-old-clothes flavor. Focusing on the scent, my head turned to the right, where my eyes tracked to a fleshy hulk, dressed like a lumberjack. He was big, easily dwarfing my two hundred pounds. Eying him, I also picked up the sour combination of tobacco, and metabolizing alcohol.

He was headed toward the express line, right where Kwan stood.

He looked to be 6'6" tall, and weighed at least two hundred and fifty pounds. As he closed on the express line, he was Paul Bunyan, relative to the other shoppers. Especially relative to the diminutive Kwan, who stood in line holding a bottle of juice and a six pack bananas.

I ignored the bump, just not important enough to have trouble over, especially considering what my senses just told me.

In the few seconds I saw him, I knew he was a drinker, not drunk, but fueled to reckless confidence by the amount of alcohol still flowing in his veins. He was short on tolerance and quick to react. Energy permeated through his body and threatened outward into the surrounding environment.

One of my early teachers had taught me to read opponents carefully. There would be days when we'd go to the market place or to the mall, and do our character studies. At tournaments, we observed how people moved, then mingled with them to learn close up. Sensei used to say he could see a mental image of an opponent's side kick by listening to the inflection in his voice. In time, different faculties evolved within me to assess and process the information my physical senses gleaned. Before long, without knowing how, I could intuit profiles of people I had been studying. Sort of like a horoscope, without the newspaper.

From the corner of my eye, I saw Kwan had noticed the man, and was already rolling his eyes skyward. I could almost hear his thoughts, "What a firecracker this character is!"

There were five people in line, with Kwan third from front. Mr. Lumberjack walked immediately to the head of the line. A large, matronly black woman faced him down, stared, then scolded, "You can't just walk in front of people, there's a line here!" She pushed on by the man, and now he was in front of the next shopper, a frail looking granny.

He was clearly riled, but he was also confused about what to do with the matron. Granny broke the confusion when she spoke up, "Why don't you go to the end of the line like everyone else, and wait your turn?"

His face flushed red, and he bore into her with a frightening stare. "Jesus," I thought, "He's going to hit her."

She timidly, but courageously, stepped forward, making it clear she would say nothing more, then waited to pay for her loaf of bread and leave.

Mr. Lumberjack, again entered the line, now between Granny and Kwan.

Kwan, turning to me across the distance, played what he called his simple Poncho character, shrugging his shoulders, turning his hands outward, and rolling the sides of his mouth down with a mockingly concernful "What do I do now?" look. He had once lived in Mexico, as well as Taiwan, and was fiercely proud of both indigenous cultures, though he wasn't above having some fun with people's pre-conceptions.

If the lumberjack had asked me, I would have told him. If he were my friend, I would have warned him without the asking. I would have said, "If you're going to get in that line, don't get in front of the short, latino looking gentleman. You'll have to take my word on this, but if you trigger his switch, he'll hurt you."

Kwan tapped him on the shoulder. "Sir, you'll have to go to the end of the line. Others are in front of you."

The lumberjack retorted, "Who's gonna make me? You?"

The line edged forward. The cashier attended the second customer, and the lumberjack laid his goods down on the checking stand platform. Not smart enough to leave it alone, he turned toward Kwan, "Listen Jose, I'm in a hurry and I don't have time to waste hanging around here in a line. If you want to protect this line and be some kind of a hero, that's fine, but as far as I'm concerned, no two bit Mexican greaseball like..."

Then I saw what I feared most. Two lightning strikes to the giant's head where the nose connected to the brow. He instantly crumpled to the floor, and his face was covered with blood. When I say instantly, I mean no one appeared to even see what happened. Immediately behind Kwan was a lady struggling with her child, who refused to exit the baskart seat. Immediately to the front, Granny was completely ignoring the rude gentleman who had frightened her just moments before. At the rear of the line two men admired the curves on a passing shopper.

I put down the tabloid, and went to help Kwan deal with the situation, when I realized he had done this while still holding the six pack of bananas, and the bottle of orange juice tucked under his left arm. Kwan stepped over the sprawling body, which lay frighteningly still on the linoleum. He mumbled, "I'm Chinese you asshole, if I were Mexican, you'd be dead!"

When I got to the register, he was paying the cashier, and matter of factly remarked to her, "You'd better call the manager and do something about him." He pointed to the floor with his chin. The cashier, leaning over the platform, looked at the sprawling mass and exclaimed, "Ohmygod...what happened to him?"

Kwan again shrugged his shoulders, did the simple Poncho and said, "I don't know Miss, he smells like he's been drinking. He just went down."

We began to make our way for the door as the cashier telephoned the manager, and there was considerable commotion as others in the line finally noticed the body on the floor. The sounds of "What happened?" or "He was standing there arguing with a lady just a minute ago." filled the air as we discretely made our way out the door. As we left the store, Granny was by the exit and winked at Kwan as we walked by.

Kwan didn't have much to say as we downed our juice and bananas headed toward Tacoma.

Thirty minutes down the road, I turned and asked, "What the hell did you do to him?"

"I don't know, I really don't know. Don't even remember, or care to remember. I would have let him have my place in line, but that wasn't enough for him. He needed some learning.

"He wanted my dignity, my self esteem. That, I could not let him have. He talked. He moved. I reacted. I hope he's okay."

"You know, you weren't nearly that sharp earlier today."

"Yeah, I knew something was coming, I felt the ripples even then. I kept asking myself what could possibly happen? But as soon as I saw him, I knew he was coming for me."

It's times like that when I believe in the cosmic guiding hand. Who knows how many dignities were sacrificed to satisfy the lumberjacks' twisted needs in the past? Who knows what combination of events made it happen that for an instant, everyone's attention was diverted elsewhere, as some huge hulk turned to intimidate a little dark skinned gentleman standing in a supermarket express line? Who would have expected the little man to be Kwan?

It's as if it had been scripted, arranged to happen precisely as it did by some knowing spirit, intent on transmitting a needed lesson to an uncaring brute, and perhaps something about restraint to my friend Kwan.

It was a long difficult day. As usual, Master Kwan pulled something out of his hat to make it memorable. A few miles further down the road, we found a night spot where we stopped for a quiet meal.

Part 3 - Actualization

Spires

Obituaries

Mason arrived 8:29 a.m., as usual.

Morning messages littered his desk, stamped from 6:30 a.m. Through the open door to his office, Claims Manager Ed Michaels overheard McKenzie's angry outburst, and motioned for him to enter.

The previous day, McKenzie had once again dropped everything to handle another, in what was becoming an epidemic of fatalities. As he met with the chief, I glanced at his desk and saw versions of the Murtaugh obituary taken from each of the local dailies.

McKenzie collected obituaries, sometimes storing them like family photos in his billfold the entire length of an investigation. He trusted "vibrations." In this instance they told of a struggling father, age 36, with four children. The deceased was a utility worker. His obituary read like a testament to hard work, outreach and self sacrificing philanthropy. His loss, another of life's tragedies.

Worlds apart from the deceased, McKenzie was a loner. His family had grown, and his "wife" had long ago jettisoned his ever stalled career. Few knew that in fact, he had never been married. During the war, he formed an alliance with a housekeeper, who then became his close personal friend. He eventually brought her to the states, and, when the political winds settled down, he intended to return her home.

Nineteen years, three children, and ten years after the political winds finally stabilized, she announced "The time to go home had come."

McKenzie understood. Had there been a "home" for him, he would have gone there long ago. The kids were in Singapore, with the mother and her re-located family, found after several long years searching after the war. All were doing very well over there. McKenzie was alone.

He left Ed Michael's office, shaking his head in disbelief. As Mason reached his desk, I heard Michaels holler from behind, "Mason, I want you to take the kid with you, it will be a good learning experience for him."

The kid was me. The year, 1986. I had just finished college with a degree in history, and after managing a car rental outlet for a year had decided to make a career change.

So after running the gauntlet of corporate schools, here I was working claims.

McKenzie came to me and said, "Pack your bags kid. We'll be gone two days. We'll head out at noon. I still have a few things I need to do on the Murtaugh file before blowing town. You're welcome to tag along if you want."

He reached for the obituaries, and immediately noticed they were set in a pattern different than how he had left them. Looking over to me, he asked, "What did you learn kid?"

"Just that it's a tragic loss. Bad things happen, even to the nice guys."

"Ponder this! Our insured's high school daughter rolls along the highway at 50 mph, going the speed limit. She becomes aware the vehicle to her front has suddenly slowed. She instinctively starts a quick lane change to her right but can't avoid contact between the left front of her vehicle and the rear of the vehicle to her front. It's a light contact, barely noticeable, but she's a good girl and knows to stop and find out if there were any damages. At almost exactly the same time, the front vehicle impacts head-on with a third vehicle in the oncoming lane. Our young lady sees none of this, pulls off to the right shoulder thinking she had just nicked the rear of the car to her front. Stopping, she is horrified when she looks behind to see two smoldering wrecks coming to a rest.

The vehicle in the oncoming lane sat folded back onto itself, the steering wheel driven deep into the front seat, impaling Andy Murtaugh."

"That should be an easy closure," I commented. "Our 16 year old rear ends the car to her front driving it into the oncoming lane where the fatal impact occurs. We're on it. How much coverage do we have?"

"Not so fast kid. What about the possibility Murtaugh fell asleep at the wheel. Maybe he caught the car to our front. Maybe that car was driven back into ours. Or, what about the possibility the car to our front suddenly turned left without seeing Murtaugh, struck Murtaugh and kicked back into our vehicle?"

I admitted, these were alternatives I hadn't considered. What McKenzie didn't say at first was he had already spoken to our driver. She was young, inexperienced, and admitted outright she never saw the front vehicle until just before the contact. She couldn't remember whether or not there was a turn signal, or if brake lights flashed on. Actually, what she said was she didn't recall seeing brake lights at all. She was alone in her car and had no injuries.

McKenzie spent most of the evening before, working in the summer twilight, documenting the skid marks, and photographing patterns of oil and debris remaining on the roadway. Even before he telephoned his friend, Trooper Wilson, he had been able to establish that only one impact had occurred between the front car, and Murtaugh's car. There were no skids from Murtaugh's car, and the impact had been clean into its left front corner. Murtaugh never left his lane, and probably died instantly.

Our driver's vehicle also left no skids, but the vehicle ahead left rubber from three tires, cutting across the center line, ending at the point of fatal impact.

McKenzie needed Wilson's help in locating the occupants of the front vehicle. According to Wilson, there was a middle aged female, and her Native American companion. They were seen at the emergency room, and released after examination. Nothing serious. He thought they would be fine.

Trooper Wilson couldn't make them out. He half-liked them, but there was something "off." As he used it "off" usually meant someone was a vagrant, a hooker, on drugs, or a pervert. He said for now, they could be found at the Evergreen Inn, as though that explained everything.

Trooper Wilson let it go with that. McKenzie could not. He was a like a coon dog, once loosed, intent on the hunt. Not that he wanted to hunt, or even that he liked to hunt, but that he lived for it. Once he felt the call, it was not in his power to let it go.

He wanted to eyeball the two, today!

Within 30 minutes of speaking with Trooper Wilson, we dropped in unannounced at the Evergreen Inn where Joseph Jay and Charlotte Collier had spent the night. Outside the door to their room, McKenzie said he tasted the lingering aroma of booze, and sex, and sensed a driving hunger for cash. It surprised me. These things escaped me and probably even Trooper Wilson. I learned later, McKenzie, whose early years were spent in the open spaces of the reservation, could instantly taste and smell things that others had long become insensitive to, even when those things were little more than unhatched needs and desires.

Closing on his quarry, McKenzie probed forward. He presented as a fellow Indian to Joseph Jay, and struck a quick but solid rapport. McKenzie pulled no punches as he explained to Jay our only goal was to protect the insured, and the insured's young daughter. I knew to keep my mouth shut. They agreed to provide their recorded report.

First off, they confirmed she had no insurance on the car. Jay then related the accident happened so quickly it was hard to describe the sequence in exact detail. McKenzie nodded his head, knowing full well truth often came wrapped in details unintentionally divulged. He listened closely.

Both Jay and Collier were clear in recalling they were headed to the Tall Trees Casino. The were not well familiar with the locale, and had just missed the casino on the right side of the roadway. The figured on turning left at the first driveway they saw and backtracking. When they slowed to turn left, they were rear ended by the 16 year old and driven across the center line into Murtaugh's vehicle. Jay assured McKenzie their brake lights and turn signals worked. He said he knew this because he had recently replaced the bulbs. McKenzie asked Collier if she had signaled to turn left. She affirmed. He then asked how far in advance of discovering the driveway had she signaled. She hesitated, then said nothing. Jay interjected that he didn't have a receipt, but he was able to provide McKenzie with "Cascade," the name of the parts shop where he purchased the replacements. Ignoring the distraction, McKenzie looked again to Collier, "Can you say under oath, with one hundred percent certainty, that you had activated the turn signal?"

She answered, "No."

Joseph Jay protested, "I'm sure you had it on."

McKenzie froze him, "She drove, she's the one who knows. Did you see her turn it on? When? How many seconds in advance of the turn? How far before the turn? Did you hear it ticking, or see it flashing on the dash panel? I'm all ears, tell me what you specifically remember."

"I'm just sure it was on when we turned, that's all I can say, Charlotte is a cautious driver, she wouldn't forget something like that."

Recognizing the two were on the move, McKenzie explained he was willing to make some sort of settlement, to include their car, a total loss, and something for injuries, but only if they would sign releases. McKenzie knew they would, even before he finished his sentence. There was another odor in the room, one unfamiliar to McKenzie, except that, whatever it was, McKenzie knew it would cost money, more than they had! These two transients would be willing to sign anything to get it. He explained how he was going out on a limb, liability remained uncertain, and there was more here than met the eye. But the young lady hit their vehicle from the rear. On that basis he could justify settlement with them, but it would have to be reasonable.

We left with two signed releases. It had cost the company $2000 total. McKenzie would catch flack for making injury payments without first obtaining medical records. Worse, the releases included the company's promise to reimburse the emergency room expenses if submitted within 180 days.

He did what was best for the insured, but he wasn't going to shaft the two transients. He could handle the heat. He dropped me off at my place to get my trip gear together.

At noon, we hooked up again at the office. Our assignment would take us to the mountain community of Spires, Washington.

As I entered the car, McKenzie looked over to me and said, "We're making a stop along the way."

"The Murtaugh case?"

Extracting his hand from his breast pocket, McKenzie handed over a folded paper. It was the signed off title to Charlotte Collier's vehicle. Now it belonged to the company.

"What secrets does the vehicle hold?" I asked.

"Tail lights," McKenzie replied. "You see, if tail lights are on when a rear end impact occurs, and the bulbs are damaged in the impact, traces of oxidation will occur, confirming they were on in fact"

"And if they're clean?"

"If they're clean, then it's no cigar."

The attendant at Jason's towing was a good old boy who wasn't going to cooperate without the benefit of some persuasion, i.e. a stick of dynamite under his chair. At first, he refused to tell McKenzie whether any cars from the accident were in the lot. McKenzie narrowed his interest to Charlotte Collier's car, but the attendant still refused to give any information, citing the privacy act.

Finally, McKenzie grabbed the signed off vehicle title from my hand, slammed it down on the desk, shouted out he was the owner of the salvage, and insisted on inspecting it immediately. If the yard wouldn't cooperate, our next stop would be to file a complaint with the State Patrol.

Though it wasn't a stick of dynamite, it was enough of an explosion to evoke a response.

"It's the black Fairlane in the second row."

We navigated through a field of mud, carefully avoiding mounds of canine scat. As we approached the Fairlane, McKenzie cautioned I should keep an eye out for the dogs. He carefully photographed Collier's car inside and out. The front was pancaked, and the right rear tail light cover was shattered from the impact. Raising his crossed fingers toward me, McKenzie optimistically looked into the open tail light, then looked up shaking his head side to side. As McKenzie photographed, I came over and saw that the bulbs had survived intact. We turned to walk away when McKenzie said, "Hang on a second." He went back to the tail light assembly and removed the bulb.

Never leaving anything to chance, McKenzie wanted to double check the unit. What he discovered was the bulb sat in a socket lined with a chewing gum wrapper.

As he exhaled, McKenzie whispered, "Joseph Jay's handiwork no doubt." The other tail light, when opened, revealed similar foil.

"What does it tell us, Mac?"

"It tells us there is at least one plausible explanation for what happened. Our inexperienced teenage driver is following Charlotte Collier, going 50 miles an hour, two to three car lengths behind, when Charlotte decides to hit her brakes. Maybe she wants to make a left turn, maybe she's braking for another reason, maybe Murtaugh drifted into her lane. In any event, she brakes and slows, but because her brake lights are not functioning, our inexperienced driver closes too quick upon her rear, and realizes the situation only as impact becomes unavoidable. She swerves right to evade, and almost does. The impact, though slight, is enough to nudge Charlotte into the oncoming traffic where the fatal collision occurs.

"But didn't you just say that the brake light appeared to be operative?" I asked.

"I don't know exactly what operative means, when the socket is lined with foil. But, we own the salvage, and we're going to have an expert extract the lamp socket, preserve it as it is, hot wire it, and run a series of brake applications just to see what happens."

As we headed out of the yard, the attendant stood by the doorway. Eying McKenzie, he said "Listen, I'm sorry I was such an ass, it's just that these fatalities get to me sometimes. I was there when they pulled the guy from the wreckage. I can't stop seeing it."

McKenzie's temper was legendary, and he always gave better than he got. But he could forgive. He stared back at the attendant, and said, "No problem. As far as I'm concerned, it never happened. Water under the bridge. From here on out, it's a clean slate."

They shook hands, and we left.

McKenzie made two calls. First to Trooper Wilson, telling him about the brake light discovery. Wilson said the fatality investigators would have a look at it. McKenzie cautioned we now owned the salvage. The State Patrol could look at it, but shouldn't touch anything until after our independent engineering firm had analyzed the circuit. He'd be agreeable for everyone doing it together if Wilson would set it up. He figured the State Patrol would probably impound the vehicle.

McKenzie winced unexpectedly. Trooper Wilson didn't like constraints, unless he was the one promulgating them. I could hear his blowback from where I sat alongside.

McKenzie then called Tim Anderson of Anderson Labs. Tim had worked with Mac on many past cases and knew exactly what Mac wanted when the situation was described. McKenzie said we'd be gone for several days, and would need a preliminary report immediately on our return, or sooner if possible.

Within minutes, we were headed to Spires.

"What's the risk angle on Murtaugh," I asked McKenzie.

"Well, we have a $100,000 liability policy on our car."

McKenzie was always good for the half answer. He took the Socratean method to its limit. Instead of answering a question with a question, he only half answered, forcing me to play Socrates by internalizing the next question, and then vocalizing my own response in the form of a hypothetical directed to McKenzie.

"So, what you're saying Mac is that our insureds, Mr. and Mrs. Hartley, have their personal assets at risk, all because of their 16 year old daughter's accident."

"Tell me kid, do you think the Family Purpose Doctrine applies here?"

I had to think for a bit, until I recalled that the Family Purpose Doctrine had something to do with whether or not the vehicle involved in the accident was a family-use conveyance. If it was, then the parents' assets stood at risk.

"Does it?" I asked.

"You tell me kid!"

Sometimes, McKenzie could be darned ornery. I grabbed the claim folder, then looked through the contents, including McKenzie's notes. Before long, I saw the vehicle was listed owned by Mr. and Mrs. Hartley, who were the named insureds, with young Helen being named as an "additional driver."

"I would say that the family purpose doctrine applies."

"Then what would you consider to be our ultimate objective on this file?"

"Get the Hartleys out of the claim, with a full and final release, while neutralizing any threat to their personal assets."

"Good thinking, Kid," McKenzie looked over and winked.

"Now kid, since you've already decided our Helen Hartley was the proximate cause of accident, what incentive could we possibly offer the Murtaugh estate to drop pursuit against the Hartleys?"

Though he didn't say it, McKenzie was signaling the estate would probably retain an attorney to go after the Hartley's, perhaps with vengeance in mind.

I thought, but turned up empty.

Then, like a glow from afar, a thought took shape in my mind. Murtaugh might have had insurance on his vehicle. If so, we would need to know whether he had underinsured motorist protection. If he did, the fact that Charlotte Collier had no insurance could work to everyone's advantage. My understanding of underinsured motorist coverage was tentative. Basically, it worked by substituting your own auto policy into the position of the person who caused your injury. In other words, your own company, for an additional premium, contracted to stand in the shoes of the party at fault. It might even be triggered if the limits of our own policy were inadequate to compensate the loss.

I looked over to McKenzie. "I think there's some sort of underinsured motorist angle here, but I'm not quite sure what it is."

"I'm not quite sure what it is either, but we have learned that Charlotte has no insurance whatsoever, and our good folks probably don't have enough. Wilson seems to think Murtaugh may have underinsured motorist coverage in the amount of $250,000. That's a lot of money these days."

I closed the file folder. Clipped to the outside were the obituaries, which I read again several times, until I began to drift from consciousness. In a perverse way, it was like counting sheep, or perhaps, reciting a mantra, until the vibration carried forth on its own, and passed through me into the road below, like a stream reaching its finger to the sea.

Killed?

Spires, Washington is a small mountain community, cradled between rolling hills in the high alpine. Except for Highway 41, Spires is virtually cut off from the rest of the world. Until the dawn of satellite dishes, it was pointless owning a TV. Its residents are descendants of the westward migrating pioneers, the ones who didn't make it to the coast, sprinkled with a "dropout" here and there, an occasional young family looking for the finer, simpler life, and of course the retirees. I always struggled with why retirees would live in a place where real medical care was still 70 miles away.

We rolled into Spires at the tail end of a long caravan of log trucks. Mountains of pulp filled both sides of the road. Along the railroad right of way to the east, fields of cut timber were being readied for transport to market.

It was a logging town. Townsfolk worked the woods, as did their forefathers. But for the addition of chain saws, and modern loaders, they worked much as their fathers and grandfathers had before them. It was backbreaking work, characterized by a frightening record of job injuries and early retirements.

But it was good work. Each day pushed one's body to its limit, and presented endless challenges to one's ingenuity and creativity. Imagine moving a 25 ton tree down a 45 degree slope with no education beyond 4th grade?

You could if you were a timberman from Spires. It was probably genetically imprinted!

Staring out my window, I could see the adjoining ridges had been cut clean. This was something new. In the old days, it wasn't considered prudent or smart to clear cut across a mountain side, leaving it looking like a mowed lawn for the next generation. Old timers would have questioned what remained to temper the frigid winter winds descending the slopes?

Controversy was brewing in the urban centers. Urbanites, while vacationing, couldn't help but to see these "eyesore" patches. It was only a matter of time before they organized political campaigns against the excessive cutting of timber, and arguing the impact of overcutting on the environment. The problem was triply compounded by the spotted owl. That indigenous resident of the old growth forest had been placed on the threatened species list, and, as a direct consequence, the old growth forests were swarming with observers quick to report any and all cutting that might impact the creatures.

The mill owners, of course, would do just fine. They had long since recouped their initial investment in land, timber and equipment. In fact, the extensive land holdings would only accelerate in value when, what was once exclusively logging land, would became recreational, with more and more urbanites bidding for weekend retreats.

Even in remote Spires, land values had doubled over the past three years.

What we saw as we entered town was the logging companies' last big dash for timber gold before operations became severely curtailed. Anticipating the unfavorable political climate, they had been operating on double overtime for the past two years, taking out any wooded tract likely to fall under the influence of the coming legislation. Unintentionally, the environmentalists, and the protectors of the spotted owl, precipitated the abandonment of normally prudent utilization practices by stimulating the mad scramble for everything that could be cut before the deadline. Old growth that might never have been attacked was gone, and a spotted owl was no longer safe in the woods, at least not from the irate lumbermen.

We didn't know it then, but it was these same issues which brought us to Spires.

At 4:00 pm, we arrived at the home of our insured, Betty Pearson. We had just enough time to pick up the background on her loss before finding lodging. Luckily, we found her at home to our unannounced call. After formalities, we sat down at the kitchen table where McKenzie proceeded to take her recorded statement.

A road weary, McKenzie instructed, "Mrs. Pearson, why don't you just take it from the top and tell us what happened as best as you recall. If I have any questions, I'll simply interject them as they pop into my head."

Mrs. Pearson understood and responded, "Well, it was about 11:30 p.m. last Saturday, and I was westbound on highway 41, heading into Spires. I was approaching the Mt. Jones cut off, going the speed limit, well, maybe a little less, about 50 miles per hour, when the body of a man appeared squarely in front of my vehicle..."

McKenzie interrupted, "Did you say the body of a man?!"

"Yes, Max Lindstrom. He's the man who was killed."

"Killed?"

For an instant, but no longer, McKenzie looked confused. I glanced down at the initial claim assignment and read a description of the loss. Single car accident, insured traveling with children on mountain road, vehicle may be a total loss, rule out bodily injury. There was no mention of a fatality.

McKenzie, back on track, asked Mrs. Pearson, "Tell me about this 'body' on the road. Was it lying in the road? Standing? Crossing the road? Walking on the shoulder? Coming towards you, or headed away?"

"I really can't answer that. I saw it just about as I hit it. It was like he was dropped from the air."

McKenzie hesitated momentarily, then said, "Where the accident occurred, is Highway 41 one lane in each direction?"

"Yes."

"Were you in your lane when the impact occurred?"

"Yes."

"You're sure of that? Were your headlights on?"

"Yes."

"Both of them?"

"Yes. The State Patrol checked them both afterwards, and they were both operative."

"How did the Trooper determine that they were on at the time of the accident?"

"Well, basically, it's impossible to drive Highway 41 at night, going the 55 miles per hour speed limit without the lights."

A few seconds of silence passed as McKenzie carefully considered his next question.

"Mrs. Pearson, I want you to describe the entire sequence of events for me, from the point in time when you first saw Mr. Lindstrom. Think of it as though you were telling me about a movie, and wanted me to visualize the entire sequence of events as you remember them."

"That will be easy," said Mrs. Pearson. "He appeared just before impact. Applying my brakes made little difference, impact occurred almost exactly as I saw him. The terrifying part came just after impact when he flew over my hood, and his head struck the driver's window, right before my eyes."

Mrs. Pearson's narration began to slow, as she struggled for the next words. "His head struck my windshield, then he flew over the top of my car. I kept my brakes on and skidded to a stop. I looked behind, out the back of my car, and saw nothing but the red and blue glow from the Alder Tavern. It was off the road and behind me on the right. The highway was empty. I mean there were no cars."

"He was alone?"

"As far as I know."

"Were there any witnesses to what happened?"

"My children were with me, that is, my 8 year old son, Michael, and my 4 year old daughter, Ruth."

"Forgive me for not asking this before, but were any of you injured?"

"No, fortunately. Unless you count the fact that I haven't been able to sleep since the night of the accident. My children saw nothing, and have pretty much been spared."

"And what happened after you stopped?"

"I saw the body on the road and ran into the Alder Tavern to get help help. They immediately summoned the State Patrol and the ambulance. The State Patrol arrived in short order and took control. I was taken to the medical center by aid car with my children, and later on that evening, the State Patrol Officer in charge interviewed me. At that time, I learned Lindstrom was dead at the scene. The Officer said he had been drinking, and that a blood alcohol test had been ordered."

"Were you told the results of the blood alcohol test?"

"No. In fact, at this point, you know everything I know."

McKenzie read Mrs. Pearson perfectly. He knew she regretted the incident, but also knew her primary concern was her damaged vehicle, which remained useless at the local junk yard. McKenzie got the identifying information on the Pinto wagon. Before leaving, he promised Mrs. Pearson we would inspect it the following day, and get back to her by late morning with our assessment. She was visibly relieved.

We left Mrs. Pearson at 6 p.m. and decided to check in at the Candlelight Inn before having a late supper. I had never had opportunity to chat casually with McKenzie, and was somewhat taken aback when, during dinner, McKenzie spoke in less than flattering terms about the company we worked for. McKenzie, saw my defensive reaction and laughed. He mocked me, saying it was impossible for me to think clearly, since I was still tainted by the unbridled ambition of youth.

When I questioned what that meant, he responded that, "All one has to do to get blind commitment and 60 hours a week from a career ambitious new employee was to point out his or her potential to oversee their peers once they had a year or two of hard work under their belt. That, and a strong positive attitude about the company almost always guaranteed success." In fact, he declared it to be a formula which never failed, just in case I wanted to take advantage of it.

I struck back at McKenzie, "But Mac, what's your gripe about success?"

To which he responded, "What's your measure of success kid? Quick, tell me!"

I didn't say it, but I was thinking success for me would mean to be an examiner at the end of 3 years.

McKenzie looked across to me and added, "I already know what you're thinking kid, but for me success is making sure people like the Hartley's don't lose their home because of some accident that fate ordained to involve their 16 year old daughter. And making sure that people like the Pearson's are spared the pain and anguish of being targeted for a fatality that could not be avoided."

McKenzie's comment surprised me.

"Whoa, McKenzie. What the hell do you mean 'Couldn't be avoided!' Mrs. Pearson all but admitted never seeing Lindstrom until the point of impact."

"Kid, even a rookie like you should know exactly what happened from what Mrs. Pearson said."

"You mean you think that you already do?"

"I know what happened. But if I'm going to keep the Pearsons out of litigation, I have to establish 'Why', and 'How'."

"You've lost me McKenzie!"

"Just think about what she said kid. While you're doing that, let's head over to the Alder Tavern, and make ourselves comfortable for the evening. We might run into somebody who knows something."

At quarter past nine, we arrived at the Alder Tavern.

By the time I returned from the washroom, McKenzie was calling me over to introduce me to Jeannie, the bartender, and three of the local loggers whose names went right by me.

McKenzie was sipping his usual glass of wine. Just red wine. It didn't seem to matter what kind it was, just so long as it was red.

Seemed that Jeannie was from McKenzie's home state of New Jersey, and for the first hour, they talked, leaving me nothing to do but watch the big screen TV. Turns out she wasn't working the night of the incident, but knew the bartender on duty had cut Lindstrom off at three beers. Lindstrom had been in a sullen mood. "We're all friends around here, nobody wants trouble."

By 11 o'clock, McKenzie was shooting dollar pool with some of the locals, and sharing war-stories with a Viet Nam veteran.

At the bar, Jeannie was telling some regulars about how McKenzie and I were investigating Max Lindstrom's death. Glancing over to me, she asked, "Is he really from New Jersey, or is that a line?"

"Cape May, New Jersey, he never stops talking about it," I responded.

McKenzie glanced back at us, saw Jeannie and winked at her. A few seconds later, he came over and asked, "Are you investigating kid, or are you watching the sports?"

Looking at Jeannie, he said, "Jeannie, I told this guy to pump you for all the information he could. How's he been doing?"

"You're from Cape May, New Jersey, and you never stop talking about it."

McKenzie, frowning, looked over at me shaking his head, "What's with you kid, we're supposed to be accountants from Duluth. I was from Cape May last month!"

He returned to the pool table.

By midnight, the weight of my eyelids tugged my head downward, until it set itself to rest on the bar. The last thing I remember was Jeannie and Mac playing pool, matching themselves against the locals.

When my eyes jerked open, the morning sun was already slicing its way through the motel blinds, dicing a pattern of stripes across my bed. My clock read 5 a.m., but I couldn't get back to sleep. I got up to peek through the blinds and saw McKenzie taking advantage of the early summer light. In the northern latitudes, we are selfish about our sunlight when we can get it. For most of us, the three months of summer meant spending every non-working moment outdoors. McKenzie was staking his claim.

Behind the Candlelight Inn ran the Ice River, so named because it served as a southern path for glacial run-off from Mt. Rainier. Also so named because it was damned cold. McKenzie had climbed over a fence into a horse pasture abutting the river. There, he was practicing some sore of martial art.

I remembered now. When I first came to the office, Ed Michaels gave me some background on each of the employees. The standout was McKenzie, who had spent a good part of his adult life traveling the far east, and studying the fighting arts. Michaels said that McKenzie was considered to be a master. Frankly, I couldn't tell. As far as I was concerned, a grown man throwing punches and kicks around a field filled with horse dung looked a bit out of place, if not silly. I decided to focus on the matter at hand, and see what I could recall from the previous day's investigation that might help our purpose.

I was already at breakfast when McKenzie pulled in with his notebook.

Not wanting him to feel self conscious about my having spied on him exercising, I asked benignly "What's on the agenda today Mac?"

"I saw you looking at me through the blinds. What did you think?"

"Were you able to get your shoes cleaned off?"

"No, I wasn't wearing any. I mean what did you think about the beautiful morning, the sunlight peeking over the hills, the rush of the icy stream, and the sounds of morning birds on the wind?"

"Sounds like Indian talk to me Mac."

Even as I said it, McKenzie stiffened.

I knew that my comment, ever so innocent, had offended that part of McKenzie's heritage which was native American.

McKenzie, long accustomed to such quips, graciously changed the subject and focused on our agenda.

"First stop is Rick's Texaco. That's where the car's at. We'll see what it has to tell us. Spires doesn't have a State Patrol detachment, but there is a Trooper Sergeant Briggs who is appended to the local police force. He was in charge of the investigation and I've already got a call into him. Midday, I've got to come back to the motel for a few hours. Michaels called yesterday and left a message for me to turn in my month end subrogation and salvage reports STAT. I'll see if we can get another night"

"But how the hell can you do those reports from out here?" I asked.

"Kid, I don't think either Michaels or the company wanted for me to ask that question."

McKenzie continued, "Then we'll drop by Spires Community Medical Center. That's where the Coroner keeps an office, and it's also where local vital statistics and records are kept. With some luck, we'll be able to access the death

certificate, and learn something about Max Lindstrom before
we contact his wife tomorrow?"

"His wife? You're going to contact his wife!" I asked.

"No kid. You are. And while you're doing that, I'm going
to be driving around town, seeing what I can learn about the
guy."

After breakfast, we headed over to Rick's Texaco. The
1977 Pinto Wagon stood alone, close to where the Ice River
raked the boundary of the junk yard. The wagon was off-
yellow, Ranchero style, with a luggage rack. From the side
where we stood, it appeared almost undamaged. McKenzie,
like a hawk descending, circled the wagon two complete
times before allowing himself to stop at the front left corner.
He pulled two cameras from the briefcase, kept the 35
millimeter, and tossed the Polaroid to me. Take four pictures
kid, one from each corner, make sure you get the whole car
in each photograph. Get a dog's eye view, low to the
ground. Then snap away at anything else you think is
interesting. I did as he instructed. McKenzie, too, snapped
shots from the four corners, but afterwards, he scrupulously
inspected and photographed every square inch of the
vehicle, starting with the roof, and ending with the tread on
the tires.

On the roof, he fingered a dent in the luggage rack. It was
on the rear bar, about one third of the way in from the
driver's side. It looked as though someone had gotten a crow
bar and attempted to bend the luggage rack backwards and
off the vehicle.

Next, McKenzie scrutinized and photographed the windshield of the vehicle, from outside and from inside.

He made me sit behind the driver's seat to "feel the vibes." It could sometimes be hard to tell when Mac was serious. He told me to "just relax and listen to the car."

"Kid, it's something any person can do. Certainly, any Indian can do. It's about time your people picked up on it."

McKenzie was getting back at me for my morning indiscretion.

As I sat behind the wheel, he shut the driver's door.

That, I didn't expect!

I looked at the dash, saw the odometer reading, and as an afterthought, logged the 38,178 on a piece of scrap paper, obviously second time around for this vehicle. My eyes dropped right and to the floor where some toys sat abandoned. Then, my gaze crept to the front passenger door, then to the right corner of the dash, then slowly to the center, where the imprint into the windshield moved to the forefront of my visual field. The impact of the head into the windshield had been hard. Hard enough to leave a web of fractures imprinted onto the glass, which drooped lazily inward from its normal surface plane. Somehow the windshield held firm.

McKenzie was photographing the spot from outside. Unexpectedly, a lump began to swell beneath my sternum, and I was beginning to sweat and struggle for air. I had to get out of the car, and as my left hand fumbled for the door latch, I found the door wasn't opening. McKenzie had locked it when he shut it. Damn him! I reached to pull the lock open, then sprung outside and walked over to sit beside the icy stream where I could breathe some free moving air.

"What did the car tell you kid?"

I turned, and McKenzie, smiling half sarcastically, half compassionately, looked down at me with a knowing glance.

I couldn't put my finger on it, but it was a dark, heavy vibe.

"Why do you do this shit, Mac?"

"It's a living kid. For the most part, it's honest and truthful. That's all. But it's not anything I want my offspring to do. By the way, I got the picture for you, you'll love the expression on your face."

We returned to the car to finish our inspection. The hood's top surface was undamaged, but the nose of the hood, just above the grille at the midpoint, had an impact dent. A section of the grill was out just beneath it, and the bumper had an impact notch further down. It wasn't a lot of damage, but enough to finish off the old Pinto.

Aside from that, the car was clean. The tire treads measured 6/32 throughout, meaning that more than half their useful life remained. The tires were not a contributing factor to the loss.

"Looks like the car's a total loss kid. While I'm back at the motel doing my month end reports, why don't you check the dealers and do up a total loss evaluation?"

I returned to the motel about midday, car figures in hand, only to bump into McKenzie on his way out.

"C'mon kid, I just got a call from Trooper Briggs. He's going to be at his office for another 15 minutes."

Shaking hands with Trooper Briggs, I thought how much he resembled Trooper Wilson in body habitus. In fact, if I mentally blanked out his voice, he became Trooper Wilson.

It didn't take long for Trooper Briggs and McKenzie to connect. Briggs was clearly sympathetic to Betty Pearson and the children. Mac was quick to point out she was our insured, and faced a potential claim from the estate of the deceased.

Trooper Briggs had not yet finalized his fatality report. Nor would he consent to a recorded conversation with McKenzie. However, informally, he talked to us at length. Trooper Briggs didn't know it, but McKenzie had the recorder running the whole time. Though a questionable practice, McKenzie had long ago learned the value of informal recordings. McKenzie's first rule of investigation was to "Preserve all pertinent information. Even if it's only for your own use." After that was accomplished, the investigator, working much like a sculptor, could chip away at the constellation of information, eliminating the non-pertinent, piece by piece, until all that remained was the "explanation."

Of course, McKenzie was not so foolish as to believe the remaining explanation was the "truth." Sometimes, the truth simply didn't exist, or the truth might be locked away in some participant's mind. Then again, sometimes the explanation was so good, that anyone who heard it, would immediately recognize it as truth. That kind of explanation won court cases. In this particular year of litigation, fourteen of McKenzie's cases went to the jury. All fourteen produced defense verdicts. He was a very popular guy with the defense attorneys.

"And you felt that the car lights were on at the time?" asked McKenzie.

"Yes sir. I did."

"Why?"

"Because Mrs. Pearson had just come through East Pass in the dark. That's one of the most treacherous stretches of road in the state, even in broad daylight. It would have been impossible to drive it at night without lights on."

"How do you know, rather, I should ask, how did you confirm she had just come through East Pass?"

"I think she said she had been visiting her sister or a friend, and was returning. I contacted the person, found out what time she left, looked at the distances involved, and, had she been driving the speed limit, she would have been positioned where the accident occurred precisely when it happened."

I looked over at McKenzie, thinking that the officer had given an answer that any jury would accept as truth. He smiled and nodded, saying nothing, but making his appreciation evident.

"And what was Max Lindstrom doing out there?"

"Lord only knows. He lives on the south side of Highway 41, about one half mile east of where the incident happened. I assume he was walking home."

"He was alone?"

"Yes."

"Then he must have come to the tavern on foot," said McKenzie.

"I don't believe so." responded Briggs, "His 1985 Ford pickup was found parked in front of the Alder Tavern; the keys were left at the bar."

"Who left them there?"

"He did."

"Was he intoxicated?"

"According to the lab people at the hospital, he blood alcohol was .21."

Both McKenzie and I knew that a level of .21 grossly exceeded the .10 level which the State defined to be legally intoxicated.

"But the folks at the bar told me they cut him off at three beers."

"They told me that too, and I believe them. Seems Lindstrom was packing a hip flask. It was nearly empty when we found him, smelled of whiskey inside."

"Sitting off to the side making his own boilermakers?"

Briggs nodded.

A period of silence passed, then McKenzie continued, "What else should I be asking you Trooper Briggs?"

Trooper Briggs looked McKenzie square in the eye, then said, "You might ask me whether I knew him from the past; whether he was dead at the scene, or conscious for any period of time when he might have said something; whether he had been drinking for any particular reason, a tragedy, a celebration; and why would anybody get that drunk in the middle of the week, knowing they had to work the following day."

McKenzie smiled at Trooper Briggs in obvious admiration. At least Trooper Briggs would have read it as admiration. In the car, McKenzie later explained he was gloating incognito because his "admiration" prompted Trooper Briggs to comment on issues that would never make it into his official fatality report.

Staring back at Briggs, McKenzie answered, "Yes! I ask all of those questions," offering a contrite smile.

"He was dead at the scene, spoke to no one, no one was present. I personally didn't know him, but in years past, he was a regular guest at the drunk tank downstairs. I checked the records, and found he hadn't been there for the past six months. In fact, it surprised a few of the guys that he was intoxicated when the incident happened. They thought he was on the wagon. Cleaned up. As to his being drunk during the middle of a work week, you might want to call over to Briar Mills where he worked. I still have to do that before I close my investigation."

We both thanked Trooper Briggs for his time, and headed out.

"Well kid, I'm gonna make you an investigator."

Seeing the puzzled look on my face, McKenzie explained, "I'm going over to the Medical Center. The coroner's in town, and I want to lock onto a copy of the death certificate. Your mission, should you decide to accept, is to proceed with caution to Briar Mills, infiltrate, and identify whoever it was that Max Lindstrom worked for. Start by asking for Max's foreman. See if you can access the man. I know this might be asking too much of you, but try to strike up a rapport with him and see what he'll tell you about Max. Think of it as a fishing expedition. Remember, if you're caught, all knowledge of your assignment will be denied. In fact, it may be denied even if you aren't caught."

I dropped McKenzie off at the clinic, and within minutes, I was at Briar Mills, standing before Malcolm Bell, Max Lindstrom's foreman up until the day of the fatality.

When he introduced himself as "Mal Bell...no relation to Ma Bell," I knew even I would be able to strike up a working rapport with this good natured old logger.

"Yeah, when I heard about Max, I really felt bad. The Lindstrom's and the Bell's both came here with the western migration. Our families chose Spires, while others, seeking bigger dreams, headed westward, founding Portland and Seattle. Our people wanted homes and peace, and a place where two healthy hands and a strong body could build a life and provide for a family. A safe place. Of course, the times have changed. Within 50 years of the westward movement, the same dream builders who owned Seattle and Portland, somehow managed to own all the land around here. I never could quite figure it out, but it gives you a lot of understanding about the way things work, and how the Indians felt."

Smiling, I thought McKenzie would have enjoyed hearing that, and promised myself to relay it to him later.

"Well, by the fourth generation, that's mine and Max's generation, all that two strong hands and a healthy body could get you were the bare essentials. Now we too are working for the dream builders, and, because we know nothing but our way of life, we're stuck. It isn't like we can pull up and go work at Boeing designing airplanes. Well, as you already suspect, I tend to see the humor in things. Max struggled. He comes from a line of drinkers, and, for years, he was sunk deeper than a 10 ounce bottom fishing rig. He'd been on the wagon any number of times, but it wouldn't be two weeks before he'd be deep into the sauce again."

"Well, what about you Mal. Did you go through it too?"

I knew it was the wrong question, because it took us off track. But, as McKenzie would sometimes say, "Occasionally, it's the wrong question that gets you to the right explanation."

Mal, his eyes twinkling, smiled back at me. "Young man, I'm sixty years old. When I was fifty, I married a woman twenty years my junior. It takes everything I got to keep up with her stone sober, and I sure as hell ain't gonna risk losing her to no whiskey devil."

"But there's one thing you should know, son. Max was my friend, and we served together in Korea. It was me who persuaded his wife Edith to draw the line about six months ago. She was gonna leave him, but we worked it out so she'd give him one last chance. Yep, if he didn't dry up this time, she was leavin' him for good."

"And what happened?

"He dried out. Couldn't believe it myself. I felt so good about it, I got him back his old job at Briar Mills. The plan was for us to open up another production line, and, with his experience, he had a clear shot at making foreman."

I had no further questions for Mal Bell. The lump had returned to my chest, and I was again beginning to find it difficult breathing. Was I missing something? I made it outside just in time. It simply made no sense, a man ending like this after turning his life around.

I swung back into town, and picked McKenzie up at the medical center. Actually, he was sitting with two nurses in the courtyard. By then, I was in a grim mood, and impatiently honked my horn for McKenzie to get moving.

Entering the car, Mac said, "Looks like you learned something kid. How about we go grab a bite, and compare notes?"

When he said it, I realized how famished I was. Not only did McKenzie work long hours, but he rarely took lunch, saying if he took an hour for lunch like everyone else, he wouldn't be able to leave the office until 8 p.m. Skipping lunch, he didn't feel guilty walking out at 7 p.m.

I nodded my head to McKenzie's suggestion and agreed.

Awakening

Over supper, we attempted to sort out what we had been able to surface. Mac was certain the answer was somewhere between us. As we relaxed before dinner, Mac shared how he had been trained in the traditional native arts. He said everyone in his clan was required to learn about the plants. They were the healers, and the knowledge they guarded was a sacred trust. His family had trained him from early youth. First, during overland trips, he and his uncles would gather plants and shrubs from the wild. Mac remembered fondly how they had spent many winter nights by the fireplace tearing the dried stalks apart. First the leaves, then the stems, and then the roots. On some plants, all parts had value. On others, one part would have value, while another would be worthless, or sometimes even harmful. The elder clansman had a sacred duty to preserve and pass on the body of knowledge, but he also had to be ever mindful his young apprentice could be seriously harmed or injured by misuse of a specimen. For that reason, they were carefully taught what not to use before learning what they could use. If for example, the value of a plant lay in its roots, the young apprentice would spend many months learning not to use the leaves and the stems. Only by default did he begin to suspect that the secret of the plant lay in the roots. In time, the child would begin to press for knowledge about the roots, questioning at every opportunity. One uncle would say they should be boiled. Another would hint they should be peeled before boiling. A third would suggest the boiling water be changed three times before the root was dried in the sun. Eventually, the tapestry would be complete, and the apprentice would be ready for the "awakening."

It was one thing to dissect a plant hypothetically by the winter fire. It was another thing to then accompany an elder stalking the plant. But to find a plant while alone was a skill unto itself. For every plant, there was an "awakening." When the young apprentice had earned the right to participate in the plant's hidden secrets, he was also asked to accept the obligation of gathering the plant for distribution to the tribe. Young McKenzie learned from the earliest this could be a daunting task. He had studied the mustards for six months, and, on his first excursion to find wild cress, had returned only with water hemlock.

His grandfather explained that until one had experienced the "awakening," there was no purpose served in attempting to gather any plant.

The child McKenzie, having experienced the humiliation of delivering a poisonous impostor to the tribe, pleaded for the "awakening." He prayed directly to the plant spirits for eyes which would see true!

Touched by his earnest desire, his grandfather took him to the Great Cedar River, where he sat the child down before a patch of watercress, growing in the clear running water.

"Always be sure to pick it above the water, so that it is pure."

The child was left at the spot for three days and for three nights. He could not leave until third sunset. It meant many hours of sitting by the creek, studying the plant. McKenzie recalled the three days inevitably grew to an eternity. During that time, he had taken countless specimens of the plant, and studied each close up, tasting the young leaves, and the mature leaves, eating the plant raw and cooked, walking the banks of the creek and identifying the patches of hemlock and wild celery which nevermore would he confuse with watercress.

By the third sunset, watercress had become a close friend that he could forever rely on to nurture his spirit in the wilderness.

McKenzie added that he had been "awakened" to one hundred and twenty seven plants. While this seemed a monumental achievement to me, he added it was fortunate others in his clan had dedicated more of their time and energy to perpetuating the ancient body of knowledge.

In a very real sense, McKenzie was doing the same with me.

He liked a long, slow evening meal. It was his period of rest, the time for recharging. As we waited for our servings, Mac pulled out a napkin and suggested we reconsider everything we knew about the accident to see where truth lie hidden within. He said we should start by going back to the beginning. Anything that seemed important, we would call a "stone." Anything that seemed of no importance, we would designate as "air."

Mac decided he would summarize the information and present each item for me to decide whether it be rightfully "stone" or inherently "air." I agreed.

"The sudden rash of fatalities."

For a second, I sat puzzled. As the waitress refilled my coffee, I blurted out "air!" She looked puzzled as she walked away.

"Spires is a logging town."

I had to think about that one. The more I considered it, the more important it seemed. Not on the surface, but in essence.

"Stone."

"The Spotted Owl."

I thought about the naked hillsides, and the media coverage in Seattle. Many of the mountain communities were turning out en masse, seeking to gather public support and awareness for their plight. Even today, a logging truck caravan bottlenecking Interstate 5 through Seattle was front page in all the papers. But I saw no connection to Max Lindstrom.

"Air."

"Mrs. Lindstrom."

I had no reaction. Looking helplessly at Mac, I shrugged my shoulders.

"Darkness."

"Stone."

"Highway 41."

"Stone."

"Alder Tavern."

"Stone."

"1977 Ford Pinto station wagon."

Surprisingly, I had to think carefully before answering this one. Why was the Pinto important? Any car could have caused the fatality. But, the Pinto bore the scars. What could they tell us? For that reason, I said "stone."

"Speed."

"It killed him. Stone."

"Weather."

"Air. It was clear and dry. A beautiful summer evening."

"Faulty equipment."

"Barking up the wrong tree. Air."

"Edith Lindstrom." It was his second reference to Mrs. Lindstrom. Did I miss something the first time?

My mind flashed back to my visit with Malcolm Bell. He said Edith was giving Max his last chance. Ah, there it was. "Stone."

"Intoxication."

The autopsy reported a blood alcohol level of .21. "Let's pass on intoxication. There's something there, but I don't quite know what it is."

"The sequence of events."

I thought of Mrs. Pearson and her description that Lindstrom had appeared just before impact, with impact occurring almost exactly as she saw him. Lindstrom flew over the hood, head first into the windshield, then spun over the roof where his body contacted the rack.

"Stone."

McKenzie tossed out the polaroid shots that we took of the Pinto at Rick's Texaco. As I sorted through them, I noticed McKenzie shuffling a new sheet of obituaries, this time from the Spires Mountaineer.

"Why did he topple, Kid? Did you think about that? I mean, how many accidents are there where the victim cartwheels over the car, front to back?"

I did have to think about that one.

"Well she was going 50-55 miles per hour Mac. That would be enough to make anyone's feet leave the ground."

"Would it? I say not always, Kid. The feet on the ground are like anchors. If that's where they were when the impact occurred, then his upper body might not have spun so dramatically."

How about this, "Lindstrom's history?"

I thought Lindstrom's history was a moot point, after what Trooper Briggs had to say, and as corroborated by Malcolm Bell.

"Air."

"Overruled. Let's make that one a stone. First he's a drinker, then he's not, then he is again. There's a story in there somewhere, and we need to find it. His history is key."

By now, we were onto our main course. Digging into his steak, McKenzie looked across at me, "His keys," pausing for emphasis, as though they were a pivotal point for the entire case.

"Air." Frankly, I couldn't see what they had to do with anything.

McKenzie elected to overrule me a second time.

"Why were they left at the bar?"

"Beats me Mac. Why the hell were they?!"

"When police investigate leapers, they consider it a possible sign of foul play if the person leaps without taking his glasses off. For some reason, persons who genuinely leap on their own seem inclined to remove their glasses beforehand, setting them safely aside."

"You're off base on that one," I told McKenzie, "Lindstrom didn't have glasses."

"You're right, but he did have keys to a parked 1985 Ford Pickup. Bet you it had less than 5,000 miles on it."

I thought a bit. "Your point, stone it is."

"Blood alcohol of .21."

"I already factored that into his history, Mac."

"Right. Then how about Briar Mills?"

"Air. Nothing to do with anything."

"Malcolm Bell?"

"Mr. no-relation-to-Ma-Bell. Air."

McKenzie was silent.

"Don't tell me you're going to overrule me on that one, Mac!"

"There's a connection there somewhere. I just can't see it. Bell comes across just too damned good, too damned positive, too damned candid and up front. It ain't natural."

"What the hell are you talking about Mac. He was the one breath of fresh air we've had this entire investigation. If he doesn't ring true, then nothing makes sense."

"Make a note Kid. Tomorrow morning, we pay Mr. Bell another visit. That'll be after you make a cold call on Mrs. Lindstrom, and get a handle on what she's thinking about doing."

"And what if she's represented by an attorney? What do I do then?"

"Find out who the attorney is, call him, and make an appointment for us to meet him tomorrow afternoon. Tell him we'll be leaving town at the close of business."

"Really!"

"Who knows? Say it anyway, it'll get his attention."

"OK Mac. If we're done with the stones, let's take a few minutes and plan our course for tomorrow."

"Well, there's one last piece to the puzzle. The coroner's report."

McKenzie had actually finagled a copy. He slid the coroner's report slowly out of the claim file. As he turned it my way, I saw in his knowing eyes that he had already somehow solved the mystery of Max Lindstrom. What was the purpose of the rest? Certainty? Protecting the insured? My continued training?

At first glance, the blood alcohol reading of .21 was officially confirmed. He was drunk by any standard. Reading further, cause of death was given as brain stem trauma, basal skull fracture. The left ankle was disintegrated, and there was a comminuted fracture to the distal right femur, as well as an open fracture to the proximal left tibia. The other notations were minor by comparison.

I glanced back at McKenzie and, looking at me, he whispered. "Stone."

Though Michaels authorized another night, by the end of the second day, Spires was beginning to wear thin. For me, the sooner we were out of there, the better. Compared to running a rental vehicle office, this work extracted an emotional toll. Part of it was the constant running around. Another part was the oppressive atmosphere that seemed to hover around us. It was as though wherever we went, a shadow tugged along. Just about everyone knew we were somehow associated with the insurance company that was investigating Max Lindstrom's death. Preceding us was the general impression that somehow, if it was at all possible, we were going to "screw" Max Lindstrom's survivors out of anything they might otherwise have rightfully coming to them. It didn't make our job any easier, and the many caustic stares left no doubt we were becoming the focus of people's idle animosity.

Small Questions, Big Answers

We finished dinner, then headed to the Alder Tavern, ostensibly to finalize the next day's plans. McKenzie's mood had darkened. On the way over to the tavern, we stopped by the hotel where McKenzie found a waiting stack of messages from Ed Michaels.

"Where is your fucking diary? When can I expect you back? Can you squeeze in a fire loss on the way out of Spires? Call me ASAP regarding a deposition you're supposed to attend!" said McKenzie as he conducted a "dime show" mimic of Michael's neurotic compulsiveness. McKenzie abhorred anything that caused him to loose center or focus. Michaels never had a center or focus. McKenzie was much like an arrow. Once released, it sailed true to its target. Michaels was fragmented, ruled by the prevailing wind, and careful to do whatever was necessary to ensure his position was covered. He was the vacuous tube through which crap passed from on high, down to on low.

To Michaels, McKenzie was a workhorse. He said as much to me on more than one occasion. A claims machine of the highest refinement. But, every compliment from Michaels was followed by the trailer that McKenzie had no management aptitude. On that point, he was wrong. McKenzie understood people to the core. If anything, it was his greatest skill. Time and again, he had managed to pull off the impossible during the course of an investigation. There was no doubt in my mind he would have been brilliant as a manager at any level in the organization. But, there was the unsolvable riddle. As long as his superiors were unable to fill the empty shoes he left behind, he would never be permitted to step out of them.

Of course, McKenzie wasn't much help. He was always the wounded Indian, ever mindful of broken promises, shattered dreams, and failed destinies characterizing the lives of those with whom he choose to surround himself. Eventually, the vibrations covered over whatever opportunities for professional growth he might have had. He was friendly, but offish. He was positive, with pronounced exceptions.

As I saw him at the bar, making moves on Jeanne, I wondered where McKenzie would be in five years time. It was absolutely clear to me he had no future with the company.

It was comical, he was day to Ed Michaels' night. When asked once about his feelings regarding Michaels, McKenzie said that he couldn't stand anything the guy did, but then again, he sensed Michaels was a man who truly cared for people, and it was far easier to work with an imbecile who loved people, than with a genius who abhorred them.

I sat with some locals and watched pro-wrestling on the big screen t.v.

Some time passed. McKenzie, was on his fourth glass of wine. It was beginning to look as though I'd have to drive us back.

Coming over, McKenzie said I should gather the "stones" and put them in my pocket, where they would be safe and accessible.

As Hambone and Demon Seed tee'd off against the Decimators on the big screen, my mind pushed the stones over, letting each roll about or bump into the others as it might...Spires is a logging town...darkness...the Alder Tavern...the Pinto wagon...speed...Edith Lindstrom...the sequence of events when impact occurred...Max Lindstrom's history...Malcolm Bell...the keys...and the coroner's report. What could be eliminated? What could not?

Something McKenzie once said began to take new meaning for me. "Sometimes the answer to the small question is the answer to the big question. Every sequence of events presents at least one small question, the answer to which will be a beacon to the truth of the large question. If you have a situation with many small questions, you are truly blessed."

In our case, we had three. First was the mystery of the keys. Second, was the mystery of Malcolm Bell. Mac was right, Malcolm Bell was too good to be true. He had conned me! Last, was the relationship between the sequence of events, and the injuries on the coroner's report.

If I could pick one question to focus my energy on, which one would it be? Is there one which would resolve all three?

"Malcolm Bell!"

McKenzie was starting his fifth glass of burgundy when I walked over. He and Jeanne were laughing outrageously, each trying to upstage the other by telling the grossest, most disgusting joke imaginable. As I approached, I caught McKenzie's attention.

"Malcolm Bell. He's the key."

Mac glanced back, pulled himself sober for just an instant, then replied, "Yes. Tomorrow, he will tell us all."

"How will we get him to do that?"

Mac let out a grudging belch, then expounded. "We'll ask him about insurance benefits available for deceased employees. Life insurance, death payoffs, things like that. And then, we'll tell him what we know about the keys to the pickup. He'll talk then!"

As he drifted back to numbness, beginning his sixth glass of burgundy, McKenzie outlined our plan for the next day. He would take care of Michaels first thing up, while I visited Edith Lindstrom. After Edith, we would both meet at the hotel, then head out to Briar Mills. He reached into his pocket and, not unexpectedly, pulled out the obituary. Studying it closely, he said "Look at that. The funeral's tomorrow afternoon, that sure throws a wrench in our plans. We might end up having to improvise."

He was telling Jeanne the only difference between an Irish wake and an Irish wedding was one less drunken Irishman, when some of the locals confronted him.

The centerpiece of the trio was Randy Maxwell. Until several days ago, Randy had been the self designated paramour of Jeannie Sloan, our friendly bartender. She had already put us on to him, with a warning to keep a distance.

It was near closing time and Randy had come to pick Jeannie up. The two apes by his side had apparently come for the ride, or for the action.

Rainwater dripped smoothly from Maxwell's beaverskin hat as he skirted past McKenzie, meticulously not glancing, almost as a challenge. I hadn't noticed it until then, but I could hear the downpour outside, and the walls lit from the strobe like flashes of summer lightning. His companions positioned themselves strategically outside the circle formed by myself, Mckenzie, Jeannie, and Maxwell, in essence, boxing in McKenzie and myself. Thunder rattled the glasses behind the bar.

McKenzie was barely able to stand, and he was still howling over his little Irish joke, when he sensed the closing envelope around us. He fell guardedly silent.

"I never figured you for the kind of slut that'd kiss ass up to shysters like these..." said Maxwell. Reaching over the bar, he snared Jeannie's wrist, and drug her upward toward where he stood alongside McKenzie.

The look in McKenzie's eyes left no doubt that even the echo of his joke had silenced. He held his tongue, but stared hard and cold at Maxwell, whose logger's grip stretched Jeannie's arm over the width of the bar, bent backwards and twisted painfully.

"Hey asshole, you're hurting her," McKenzie hollered as he stepped hard toward Maxwell.

Instantly, the point of a knife was pressing underneath McKenzie's chin, lifting him high onto his toes. Anymore pressure would have drawn blood. Jeannie freed her arm, facing the two in panic.

"Go ahead Dickweed, give me a reason. There's not a person in this town would say I did wrong by taking you out right now. Then the next time some insurance company sent a hired gun to screw simple folk out of what was theirs, they wouldn't send a drunk hole chaser like you."

"That's right! He's drunk!" I shouted, "That's what they'll say, You slaughtered a drunk helpless old man who threatened no harm."

Jeannie lunged over the bar and slapped the palm of her hand hard into the front of Maxwell's face, backing him off of McKenzie. He stumbled backwards, blood already dripping from his face from where she made sure to rake her fingernails. When Maxwell regained his composure, and advanced toward Jeannie, she was across from McKenzie, with her hand on the bar. There she fingered a .380 automatic.

The sight of it stopped Maxwell cold, "Choosing sides bitch?"

Jeannie's hand rose from the bar, her .380 now pointed squarely at Maxwell's chest, "Get out of here. Get out of my life, you worthless piece of trash. Don't ever come in here again, or your two goons will have to drag you out dripping shit. And there's not a person in this town wouldn't say you didn't have it coming."

Maxwell and the boys backed out, still focused on McKenzie and me.

"You two are poison," Maxwell scowled, "You don't do good for anybody. You take from the poor and needy and give to the fat and bloated. You don't belong here. If you're not gone by tomorrow sundown, her toy gun won't make a damn bit of difference."

"Thank God they're gone," I whispered to Jeannie as McKenzie's head dropped to the bar.

"I could have dropped the mother," slurred McKenzie.

"Yea Mac, you could have dropped the sucker, and we'd all be in the hospital," I responded.

Mac, defending his honor to Jeannie, said, "The kid doesn't know shit. I could have dropped Maxwell so fast, he would have forgotten he was even holding the knife. There's something else Jeannie, I would've dropped him because he's a liar. You're no slut, and we're no shysters."

"I know big guy," and looking over to me, she motioned for help as she got under McKenzie's arm and lifted him from his seat.

A heavy air of finality enveloped our morning planning meeting. For once, McKenzie skipped breakfast. Along with his morning messages was a memo from Tim Anderson to the effect that he ran 500 cycles on Charlotte Collier's brake lamps, and they failed to light 50% of the time.

McKenzie immediately recognized the break that might keep the Hartleys out of litigation.

He briefed me on how to play the information to maximum effect. Then he said that prior to coming down for breakfast, he spoke with Ed Michaels and talked him into switching the Hartley file to me for final handling.

I told Mckenzie I would take it, but only if I had his expert guidance on what to do.

McKenzie had heard from Michaels that the estate had chosen Thomas Winslow to represent the fatality claim.

McKenzie further explained that, while we were in Spires, his stand-in at the office confirmed Murtaugh's vehicle did have Underinsured Motorist coverage.

"Do you know how to play that hand, kid."

"I'm not sure Mac. We hit the Collier vehicle, and push it across the center line into the Murtaugh vehicle. The Collier's brake lights were probably on at the time, but maybe they weren't. We're not sure. Statistically, it's about 50/50 they were on at the time. Doesn't that hang us?"

"It's like setting up a sting, kid. When you get back into town, contact Thomas Winslow and tell him that we found the brake light sockets on the Collier vehicle to be lined with tin foil. Add how you believe this unusual arrangement caused the brake lights to be functionally inoperative at the time, and stress this was the real probable cause of Helen Hartley's failure to detect the suddenly slowing vehicle to her front. Then after you tell him that, remind him the Collier vehicle was uninsured, you have a statement to that effect, which you'll be glad to have transcribed with a copy for his file."

Then it hit me!

"Jesus McKenzie. I think I've got it, and I'm trying to verbalize it, but I'm not sure if I can."

"Do the stone and air technique, kid."

"OK Here goes. The Hartley's have liability coverage to $100,000...stone! Collier has no insurance on her vehicle...stone! The brake lamp sockets were lined with aluminum foil...stone! Tim Anderson has determined that the brake lights worked only 50% of the time..."

"Now, don't rush kid."

"Air! I mean to us, it might be important, but relative to the sting, it's air. We are better served leaving the significance of the foil lined brake lights subject to the conjecture of the estate attorney, than we are sharing the facts of Tim's analysis in free discovery."

"God kid, you're almost getting the hang of it!"

But then, my well ran dry. I knew I was close to something, but simply could not find a peg on which to hang my hat.

"The last step kid is that you offer the $100,000 liability money to the estate, in exchange for a full and final Release of all Claims against the Hartley's."

"But what incentive is there for the estate to go for it, especially in light of the fact that the Hartley's have personal resources which might be open to attack as excess over liability limits."

The gleam had finally returned to McKenzie's eyes when decisively, he responded , "Because there is a legitimate question as to whether Helen Hartley ever caused the accident to begin with."

I felt like I was locked into some sort of Zen test at this point. McKenzie simply sat silent, buttered my hijacked danish, poured through the coffee and began to read the morning newspaper.

Then it hit me like the wash from a fire hydrant.

"So, the estate will do better accepting our offer of liability limits, and then arguing for the limits of their own Underinsured Motorist Coverage, than it would do pursuing the Hartleys for moneys over and above their basic liability coverage."

"Yup, pass the comics will ya? Don't forget to press Winslow for a covenant not to sue. He'll have to get their own insurance company on board for that, but that's his job, not ours."

Suddenly, I realized we had gone through our entire morning Pow Wow without once mentioning Max Lindstrom and Edith Lindstrom.

As we knocked down the last of the coffee, Mac glanced casually over to me and said, "Go on out to Mrs. Lindstrom's house and see what's on her mind. Depending on what she says, we'll know whether or not we have to see Malcolm Bell."

"But what if she's represented by an attorney."

"If she is, then we'll just have to go see him too."

I was back within the hour. When I went to the Lindstrom residence, Mrs. Lindstrom was at the funeral home. The person I spoke to gave me the card of local attorney, Michael MacSparron. I called the number on the card, spoke with Michael, and surprisingly, was able to arrange for a meeting later in the afternoon, which, he promised, would be attended by Edith Lindstrom. He added that she would make her exact position known to us at that time.

McKenzie received the news warmly, "That gives us the time that we need to nail this down Kid. Like I said yesterday, now we have to improvise."

McKenzie and I drove out to the funeral home, where the viewing was underway.

Randy Maxwell and his cohorts were there, and their cold stares soon nudged the rest of the crowd, which, before long was focused more on our presence than on Max Lindstrom, lying in state.

"I don't like this Mac!"

I spotted Mal Bell, who twinkled his fingers in the air, shyly throwing a greeting, then seeming to regret doing so at the same time.

McKenzie sensed immediately who the reticent stranger was. Walking up, introducing himself, he said, "Mr. Bell, My name is Mason McKenzie, and I need to ask you a few more questions, beyond what my colleague asked you the other day. Can we step outside for just a few minutes?"

Bell looked to the front at who could only be Edith Lindstrom, stoically fixed in position, staring only at the coffin.

"How had it all come to this?" her puzzled stare seemed to say. Did the others also feel this? I glanced at McKenzie, who stared intently at Mrs. Lindstrom, then focused again on Mal.

I followed Mason and Mal outside, and found them sitting beneath an ancient cedar.

Mason broke the ice, "Mal, I came here to share some thoughts with you, because I know it will mean something to you that it would not to anyone else."

Mal Bell looked back at Mason, intently.

"What happened to Max Lindstrom was tragic, and I can't help that. But whatever script he was living within has passed, and he took that turn willingly."

Mal's left hand began to play at his chin, as he studied McKenzie more closely.

"You see Mal, I know how Lindstrom died, but, I'm not sure why he died! The funny thing is I think you know how he died too, but I also think you're one up on me, because you know the why! The problem I have is I can't let it rest. If my only option is hanging Betty Pearson out to dry, that won't wash. She's my insured, I protect her. I'll go the distance with that."

"It's like this Mal," McKenzie came closer, almost whispering into his ear, "You and I both know Max Lindstrom committed suicide."

Mal Bell's head sank down into his hands, seeming as though, but for the platform of his palms, it would have dropped like a tree cone to the ground.

"I believed that Max was on the wagon, just like you told my colleague, but this went hard against the fact that on the night he died, he was drunk on his ass, having to go to work the next day. That's what I couldn't figure out. Leaving his car keys with the bartender was an unmistakable sign. He was leaving them and the pickup for whoever would survive him. No more and no less. He may have been drunk to numbness, but from his long experience with alcohol, the rest of his plan was still clear in his head. He left the bar, positioned himself in the darkness beside the road shoulder, and, at the opportune moment, ran out onto the roadway, jumping at the last second into the path of the Pearson vehicle. Because both of his feet were off the ground, his body toppled hard, head into the windshield, feet over the top, then off of the luggage rack. Yes. Suicide it was. But why? Especially if things were looking up like you said they were? They were looking up, weren't they Mal."

Proudly, Mal straightened himself from his folded position. He didn't look so cooperative anymore, so unsophisticated, or so amiable.

"You son of a bitch. Why do you have to bring this out. Especially at a time like this."

McKenzie sat silent, then added "It would help Mal, if you would fill us in on what it is I'm trying to reconcile."

Nodding slowly in affirmation, Max opened up, "Yeah, we hired Max at the mill, and for a couple of months he was just fine. Then one day, I saw him sleeping mid-shift, on top of a stack of chips. He was drunk and passed out. No one knew about this but me and Max. It was our secret. I told him if he could get his act together, I'd forget it, but that if he couldn't, I had no choice but to fire him. Then there was a second incident, when Max was working on the green line. Then there was a third, at the monster saw. He could have been killed. I didn't want my silence to be the cause of his death, or anyone else's. No way. I saw the writing on the wall. Max had gone down again, and so long as I covered for him, I was in danger of going down with him too. He had let

231

everyone down. Last week, I took Max aside, and told him that if I ever caught him drunk on the job again, I would fire him, no more chances, no other considerations at all. Just fire him! Two days later, he was drunk on the timber line, with no wood feeding through. I took him out of the unit, told him what I thought of his idiocy, and fired him on the spot. I walked him to his time card, told him to punch out, no more work, no more benefits, no more welcome at the plant. You're on your own Max. Have a good rest of your life, end of story."

"So that's why he got drunk. There wasn't any work on Thursday morning, and then, sometime during the course of the evening, he hatched his plan to end it all by a random encounter with a vehicle on Highway 41."

"He did it for the insurance," said Mal.

"Insurance?"

"Yea, part of our benefits package is a $50,000 life insurance policy. It would have been canceled with his formal discharge tomorrow. But, I guess the suicide makes it all pointless."

"Not necessarily Mal," responded McKenzie, "My job is to protect the Pearson's. Frankly, I'm not concerned with whether or not Max Lindstrom's estate is entitled to the benefits of a life insurance policy. Unless they make a big stink out of the Pearson incident, I think I can let certain things slide."

"I'm not sure I track Mr. McKenzie," responded a puzzled looking Mal.

"Listen Mal! Me and the kid are meeting with Mrs. Lindstrom and her attorney later this afternoon. It might not hurt for you to talk to Mrs. Lindstrom, and let her know that so long as there's no liability claim against the Pearson's, then my investigation leaves town with me. She'll be on her own with the life insurance company."

Mal Bell nodded silently.

Wrapping Up

The meeting with Edith Lindstrom and attorney Michael MacSparron occurred almost as an afterthought.

McKenzie's argument was convincing, if not foolproof, and all present at the meeting recognized the truth when it stared them in the face. Edith Lindstrom arose, and over her attorney's objection, spoke out to McKenzie, "Mister McKenzie, I know you and your colleague haven't received the best reception since you've been in our community. I want you to know here and now that none of that was my doing. I spent nearly 40 years with Max Lindstrom, and though I loved the man, I'll be the first to say that a cross has been lifted from my shoulders. I don't know how it is for you and your fold, but here in Spires, we're at the end of our rope. It won't be long before lack of employment forces the last of the pioneer families out, probably to live in some bleak hovels, lost forever in Seattle, Tacoma, or Portland, while the developers reach in to turn the last of our breed into real estate agents, apartment managers and gas station attendants. When you leave town today, you'll have no ill will from me. You did your job straight and true, and if you hadn't, I would have followed Mr. MacSparron's counsel and caused a lot of unnecessary hardship for Mr. and Mrs. Pearson. Go ahead and close your file. If I deserve the life insurance proceeds, I'll get them. If not, I won't. You do what you want with your investigation."

We finished up at attorney MacSparron's office, then headed back to the motel and packed. As usual, McKenzie had a slough of messages from Michaels piled in his box. He picked them up, then crumpled them into the first basket we passed. Unread.

Mac wanted to say goodbye to Jeannie, and before I had time to raise objections, her luggage was packed into the car, and she had displaced me in the front seat. Mac was right of course, it was a tailspin for her if she stayed in Spires.

As we gassed up on the edge of town, a 4x4 Blazer pulled into the service mart and Jeannie's shocked expression told me without looking that Randy Maxwell had somehow found us. McKenzie stepped out of the store, saw Maxwell, and, diplomatically, cleared a path. I hoped Mac would get to our car before all hell broke loose.

But it was not to be!

With two giant steps, Maxwell was upon McKenzie, and with one paw, spun Mac hard around, "You're still in town asshole. It's sundown!"

"Maxwell, I've got no bad blood with you, and I can live with last night. All I want to do is get out of town in one piece. If you'll look at the horizon, you'll see that the sun isn't quite down yet, so, I'm still doing everything I can to meet your deadline. Besides, I met with Edith Lindstrom and her attorney today. You probably haven't gotten the word yet, but I'm a good guy again."

It was too late for diplomacy. Maxwell spotted Jeannie in the passenger's seat, charged around to her side of the car and screamed through the closed window, "Where the hell you going you two-bit whore? Open the door before I break the window and drag you out!"

McKenzie got into the car, started the engine, and with his hands griping the steering wheel, stared at Maxwell in utter amazement. "Jeannie, this guy's positively dangerous."

Maxwell looked thru to Mac, "Cut the engine!"

"Let's get out of here Mac," said Jeannie, still not acknowledging Maxwell.

"Yea Mac, let's get the hell out of here," I chimed in.

Now closing in on Mac's side, Randy Maxwell lunged toward the open driver's window, his right hand shooting straight for McKenzie's coat collar as his left positioned for a full choke. His two buddies were approaching fast, one on each side.

In one motion, McKenzie's right hand reached above Maxwell's arms and out the window, locked onto Maxwell's free-hanging hair, and drug him head and shoulders into the car. Maxwell's left arm was pinned useless against his body, his right arm flayed wildly, reaching for the rooftop.

Meanwhile, McKenzie had both his arms leveraged onto Maxwell's head, pressing it hard against the steering wheel, sounding the horn, quick freezing Maxwell's two friends, as McKenzie dropped the car into reverse, floored and spun-turned, using the wheel like a tourniquet against Maxwell's neck as his head dipped to the 6 o'clock position. I could see Mac's knees leveraging upward, and wondered how he had even thought to do such a thing. We accelerated westbound onto Highway 41. Maxwell's arms groped wildly trying to no avail to find McKenzie. It had only been seconds, but the logger was turning blue and dripping blood out the nose. McKenzie spoke softly at Maxwell's frozen head, whose labored breathing heaved in counterpoint, "Randy, my patience is beginning to wear thin."

Our speed was approaching 80 mph, and Mac was drifting close to the center line, with passing logging trucks barely missing Maxwell's free floating legs, suspended from the side of the vehicle.

"I'll say this just once Maxwell. To me, you're dead. That means I will never see you, or hear from you again. If you ever surface in my life, or if I hear of your name, or even if I bump into you by accident, you'll pay a price that your neanderthal mind can't possibly fathom. Remember me, remember what I said, and keep away. And forget Jeannie Sloan, you'll live a lot longer."

Maxwell was foaming. I screamed, "Jesus Christ Mac, you're killing him," at which point, Mac slammed hard on the brakes, not quite stopping, then catapulted Maxwell out the window. Turning hard away, he hollered, "It's sundown Maxwell, and I'm out of here!"

We accelerated into the setting sun, heading due west. I looked behind to see what became of Maxwell, but saw only that Spires receded in the distance.

Two Masters

The audible thud drew the attention of all nearby. In ceremonial gown, the Archer stood to the left, while eyes of admiring onlookers locked onto the target, positioned fifty paces to the right. The arrow extended perpendicular from the face, it's brilliantly colored feathers shimmering in the late afternoon sun.

It was a magnificent shot, centered perfectly within the ring of concentric circles.

Spellbound, the still gathering crowd milled silently about for several moments, whispering in awe before exploding into complimentary applause. Having observed competitions throughout the long day, they had grown accustomed to inconsistencies in levels of skill and trueness of aim among the various competitors. A large number had already departed, not expecting better than earlier. Only the most dedicated waited to see the Master's performance. This proved well worth the test of their patience.

His first effort set the standard for the entire day. No one had shot so true, and with such level of confidence and quietude. All eyes turned back to the Master, as he reached to draw a second arrow. Again, briefly, he became the center of interest as all focused on his drawn bow. For a fleeting moment, time stopped as he remained still, the distant target a mere afterthought. With no perceptible movement on his part, the arrow exploded from the bow, landing yet again square center on target, impinging on space already claimed by its predecessor.

This time, there was no explosion of applause. The crowd stood stunned, and silent. What first appeared perhaps to be luck so much as skill, was now beyond question and circumstance. Some suspected trickery, doubting what they witnessed to be humanly possible. With no regard to their thoughts or reaction, the Master began to unstring his bow.

Glancing one last time at the target, he turned, then proceeded to exit. He had made his statement with two shots.

One of the foreign spectators leaned to a translator asking what would be next.

The translator replied, "Nothing."

A large man, so large in fact he physically dominated the translator, approached and spoke loudly, "We waited these long hours because we were promised a demonstration by the Master, and two shots fired at a target is hardly a demonstration by anyone's measure. We paid good money to be here! Where is the rest of the show?"

Not the least intimidated, the translator responded, "You have witnessed a miracle!" His incredulous look bordered on disrespectful, at least by the standards of his people. He knew it, but felt it necessary. A fool is a fool in any culture, and sometimes needed to see himself in the eyes of others.

The large man laughed, "What miracle? He fired two shots and hit the target. Granted, he hit the target square in the center, but miracle? I think not." Patience now stretched, the translator responded, "Consider this. The first shot was impeccable. Only one thing could possibly top the first shot, and that was the second. The miracle is the Master intended to do what he did both times. Once that was accomplished, he could offer nothing further to demonstrate or prove his skill. One yang, one yin. The circle complete."

"I don't get it," the large man said as curious others gathered around, "What was accomplished, where was the entertainment, what he did wasn't enough, we're here for the show. Bring him back out, we demand an encore."

Looking the large man square in the eye, the translator answered, "For many, the first shot was enough. It was undoubtedly the best shot of the entire day, and he owed nothing further to anyone. The second shot was his proof the first shot was no accident. That is the way of Masters. They are not concerned with entertainment, nor are they concerned with your 'show', whatever you might think that to be."

The answer seemed to satisfy most, some nodding in agreement as they dispersed. The large man ended standing alone, as if waiting for more attention and some degree of satisfaction. Even the translator turned away.

Whether fact or legend, the story of the Master Archer speaks directly to the core of what constitutes the best proof of truth.

Now suppose for a moment you are a man of unique awareness, hoping to awaken the same within those about you. You will grapple with the ultimate fear, death itself! The prescribed winding up for every mortal, lights out, the end of everything. You have accepted the challenge, overruling the reservations even of your closest associates, and have chosen to demonstrate victory over death by raising the deceased Lazarus, who has been cold in the sepulcher four days. Like the Archer's first arrow, it is a singular statement of message, "There is life after death!" But is it enough? Will it convince the doubtful? Won't he still eventually die anyway? What about the arrogant man sure to be in the audience? Does it answer all questions about who you are, and what ultimate message you deliver? Once past the excited awe of onlookers, and apart from drawing the ire and skepticism of authorities, can it be certain whether any message is perceived at all, except perhaps a wonderful stunt has been executed?

There is a common link between the two. Their focus on the absolute is certain and complete, even to where they have superseded our limited notions of what is life, what is death, what is possible, and what is reality. The first Master demonstrates his ability to explode from the void to produce a perfect outcome in our plane of consciousness. Right before our eyes. The second Master demonstrates there is a place we go after our biological lives conclude, but to call it "death" is misconstruing the reality.

What remains for the second Master is the final "proof."

Unlike the Archer, he doesn't have the option of raising Lazarus a second time. A sour joke, doing so would appear even more like a stunt than the first occurrence and if anything, would create doubt regarding the ultimate message; triumph over death is indeed possible.

So, we have the second Master, the purported "son of God" meticulously orchestrating his own death, setting stage for sake of assertion and final reflection. He is tortured, crucified, speared, declared finished, there could be no doubt. Then placed into a gifted previously unused sepulcher from which he rises. For good measure, the tomb is protected by a stone front, sealed under authority of Rome, and at all times under heavy guard. Could Houdini have prepped it better?

In the first instance, he ordered "Lazarus, come out." In the second instance, he was already dead going in. No one called out, no one expected anything. Yet he is reported to have risen. Consider this. Where was he? If he was truly dead, how could he have returned? What did he do during the interim? What was the purpose of the return? Who gave the command to arise? No one heard it. Where did the command emit from? What did he prove by all of this? Won't he too die anyway? The point?

243

Like the matter of the archer, perhaps nothing more than a gift, both making indisputable that which is possible. The fulcrum is simple and cuts to the bone of all human experience and belief. What we think of as death is not the termination or conclusion of existence. Nor should it be home to our fears. In like fashion, what we think to be life is not the substance or act of existence we are persuaded to think it is. It's not about the constant pursuit of pleasure, daily hours spent on social media, the game score, or the concert. Nor is it about who we think we are, what others make of us, or all the messages confirming our deficiencies, bombarding us with how we need what someone sells to look better, be better, feel better, or become more secure from fear and the unknown. Somewhere in between is the direct experience of the eternal. From that spot, all is possible. Find it! Both Masters knew this. The dead rise, and the deceased return. The arrow strikes the target, and its companion follows closely behind. All conducted right before our eyes. Don't plead for the rest of the show. You've already gotten it.

In ancient Rome, many tombstones were inscribed with the words "Non fui, fui, non sum, non curo (I was not; I was; I am not; I do not care)." It makes one wonder, don't you think?

Tacoma Spring

This time of year, the birds come.

I went to a flea market, and saw a mammoth display of birdseed. I always wanted to feed the wild birds. Actually, not so much feed them, as to spy on them. Like watching visitors from different worlds as they descended into my back yard to feast and party.

In the past, bird feeders proved too expensive for my limited means. Now, they were selling at bargain basement prices. Who could resist the temptation? Such a deal, and only an hour's wage for a 20-pound box of wild bird seed. I bought two feeders, 20-pounds of seed, and all was set. With great delight, and high expectations, I readied the feeders.

The first day, nothing.

The second day, a fearless sort ventured into what for him, could very well have been a trap. Life certainly poses its risks, but then again, it was a long journey north and we were talking about store bought, grade A, premium quality wild bird seed. Sunflower, corn, millet ... yum. Why even I was tempted!

He feasted!

The fill level on the feeder dropped a notch or two, and in direct proportion, the chest and belly of the delicate creature began to inflate. After consuming what certainly was his body weight, he jumped off the feeder perch, expecting to fly easily away. His body dropped a full six feet, nearly touching ground, before the accelerated thrust of his wings lifted his over limit load skyward.

Next day, all the seed was gone. I suspected something big was underway!

The day after was Saturday, which I had already allocated in its entirety to bird watching. In the mid morning I loaded both feeders, then sat in a corner of the yard with an uncorked bottle of premium dry burgundy. As an afterthought, I jerry rigged two old juice bottles into hummingbird feeders and filled them with sugar solution. I planned to sit it out, wait, and experience the unexpected.

Before long, they came. I mean birds. Possibly hundreds of them. Big and small, yellow, red and blue, humming and chirping.

Someone had put out the word.

I watched for hours, refilling the feeders when necessary. By noon, they had eaten a full five pounds, and weren't showing any signs of letting up. I was on my second bottle, matching them drop for seed.

A cat passing by glanced jealously over, envying my perch.

Entering my head from the void, a musical montage of birds, children, barking dogs, and *All You Need Is Love* emerged on the warming breeze. In retrospect, it was probably there all along, but I hadn't noticed until the accumulative effect of wine worked its magic. The birds obviously relished the fare. I wondered if people acted this boisterously in restaurants, but, being people, couldn't allow themselves to take notice. I decided they did not, rather than risk harsh crossings with my own kind.

I saw a kite in the sky. Three boys in the distance had finally managed to get it aloft. Their sisters sat nearby, and their own voices, floating on the wind, told me they were playing house and fantasizing their lives as they hoped them to become.

I sat my glass down in the grass by my foot. A worm stretched along in harmony to the concert. Above him, a dandelion gave shade from the sun. A flash of yellow at the top, and just as I saw it, thousands more magically blanketed the lawn around me.

I abandoned my seat to lie on the ground. It was soft and sweet. I closed my eyes, and my consciousness dropped away the accumulated years of baggage my life had become. For a few moments, I was once again flying a kite and living in the world of dreams where life was free and delicious, and without risk.

Spring had finally arrived, and winter's darkness had departed for the moment!

Epilogue

The Water Principle

It's nature's way. Water always finds the most efficient path. It can't do otherwise! If only we could emulate.

But to where? Can anyone say? Is it for us to puzzle over its ultimate goal or objective? I prefer to leave those concerns to the turns of distracted imaginations.

Still, as it speeds along to where ever, barriers and obstacles constantly arise to trick or impede its flow. Who can say why? They're just there. Same with water as with us. Many call it "Life."

The inherent efficiency of what unfolds may not always be apparent. Getting to the heart of the water principle obliges reflection on several levels, thinking three dimensionally if you will.

On its surface, water most often represents "gentle" energy, always yielding, soft, pliable and comforting. Can you believe this very gentleness makes it the great shaper of nature?

Just as water chisels mountains and canyons with its casual lingering embrace, our first tier of understanding invokes the conceptual contradiction that even seemingly yielding to challenges, we surround and adhere to embrace them and their directed energy, in the end, eroding their focus. When they thrust, we recede, when they retreat, we fill the void. This is the water principle. Though we are apart from our antagonists, who or whatever they might be, like water, our movements become one with that which would stymie us. Seamlessly. Each apart, yet each integral to the movement of the other. In the end, there is only the one. We know what's going on, it doesn't matter that others don't. No different than whittling down the opposition. They look for resistance, but find only an empty jacket. Patience, fortitude and compassion work their magic.

The next level addresses the matter of flow. Water possesses the freedom to flow in any direction, and it knows it. "Knows it?" you ask. Well, if it didn't, it wouldn't get anywhere. As it stands, for water there are unlimited choices and possibilities. The key however is "What's the best choice?" There, it excels. Without fail, it finds the most expeditious path, regardless of the obstacles confronted. It seems water can not make the wrong choice about flow. There's a lesson in that.

We strive for the better. Somewhere out there lies the great success. Or so we think. For some, enlightenment, For others freedom, or awareness or perhaps power, wealth, dominance. Not unlike water in its endless quest for the sea.

There are innumerable options and endless obstacles and choices. Like water, the finest among us conduct our search with true hearts and impeccable spirits. With an empty mind, detached from the constraints of time and difference, any path undertaken will bring us closer to our goal. As with water, issues of success or failure, correctness or incorrectness, power and dominance become meaningless. If the heart is true and the spirit impeccable, the road will be right. We can't control outcome, only the orientation of our hearts and the commitment of our spirits. All else loses meaning. All else is distraction.

The final level of insight is where we become exactly as water, totally fluid and perfectly integrated with our surroundings. Thoughts about victory and defeat are questions pertinent to "ego" and "self." Like mountains and canyons over time, these too dissolve on our arriving at the "experience" of the water principle. We're not talking about understanding anymore. Understanding becomes just another bit of stuff in the way, another something passed along the course to awareness. We don't experience the water principle by "understanding" it. It's all in the doing. We either do it or we don't. There are no alternatives to simply getting it by doing it. When one experiences the water principle, the "one" who "understands" the water principle no longer exists and is of no consequence. Pursuit of victory and fear of failure reduce to mere whimsies when one becomes like water and responds with the appropriate solution for every situation. Once the principle has been mastered, there can be no wrong move. It's about staying true to self, and nature.

So when describing the characteristic that one following the water principle always makes the correct choice no matter what he or she decides to do, we are faced with a paradox. How is it possible that in becoming perfectly fluid and one with the flow of the universe, one makes the "right" move no matter how he or she moves? To the uninitiated, it would seem being locked into the "perpetually correct" steals from the mindfulness of choice and threatens one's very existence. The reality is distinctions become meaningless, and debates over freedom of choice, and what is right or wrong are left to the philosophers while the enlightened flow on by unaffected by the obstructions.

Consider the English nursery rhyme and one of its many variants. Who do you think has it right?

> Row, row, row your boat
> Gently down the stream
> Merrily merrily, merrily, merrily
> Life is but a dream

or

> Row, row, row your boat
> Gently down the stream
> If you see a crocodile
> Don't forget to scream[3]

---

[3] Johnson, B. & Cloonan, M. (2009). Dark Side of the Tune: Popular Music and Violence. Aldershot: Ashgate. p. 98. ISBN 1-4094-0049-2. In Bean, where Rowan Atkinson (Mr.Bean) and Peter MacNicol (David Langley) also used this parody singing in the film. On February 23, 2004, I had the opportunity to hear Dick Gregory speak at the University of Puget Sound. To my surprise,

we shared one particular thing in common. He was completely enamored of the rhyme, as I too had become over time. I seem to remember him saying, "It's everything anybody really needs to know," or something to that effect. He didn't have to catch his plane until the middle of the night, so he lingered long beyond his allotted time, ending up on the front steps of the Kilworth Chapel. He was very generous with his insights and shared many stories. In retrospect, the evening flowed very much like a dream.

Acknowledgments

The book cover image was taken from a photograph by my good friend Bobbi Youtcheff. Bobbi has a remarkable eye for capturing the moment, and the original image was entitled "Favorite Restaurant." She shared the back story. The establishment was indeed her favorite restaurant, a cozy little hideaway off the beaten track during her sojourn in Japan.

When she first shared it with me, I asked what made her take the shot looking through the window at night. She answered it was already her favorite restaurant, but something magical happened as she walked by one evening. She peered through the window and felt anyone could find peace and comfort within, as well as a good meal. She took the shot, hoping to capture the moment, and feels she did.

It was the window that hooked me, and that became the cover for *Returning to Center*.

The artwork within was done by Renee Knarreborg. When she wasn't attending to electric power plants and demands of life, Renee somehow found time to listen to my story lines and my pleas she work highlights into the images you see. She kept it simple, pencil or ink on paper. The colors in the E-book were added by myself from a 16 color palette at a later date.

Many thanks to my friends who volunteered to read, and comment, their feedback made better things happen. They are Bob Kirschenbaum, Sid Olufs, Bryan Smith and Bobbi Youtcheff. The mistakes and oversights are all mine.

I am indebted to the many masters who have befriended me over the years and who took great care sharing their knowledge and remarkable skills with this stumbling pilgrim. Foremost among them, the incomparable Isidro Archibeque, whose teachings and exploits I have attempted to document and preserve at:

www.ironcrane.com

Lest any others be unintentionally overlooked, my complete lineage can be viewed at:

http://www.ironcrane.com/IC_Flowchart_Color.jpeg

About the Author

Billy Ironcrane is the writing and music performing pseudonym for Bill Mc Cabe, a lifelong explorer of life's experiences and unending surprises. Raised in inner city Philadelphia during the 1950's and 60's, he partook in the revolutionary currents of change, protest, activism, and idealism which characterized the era. While a teen, he spent summers on the Jersey coast hawking newspapers, tossing burgers and exploring places like Wildwood and Atlantic City where he encountered flea circuses, Gene Krupa hanging between sets at the Steel Pier, petrified mermaids and the fabulously wealthy promenading the boardwalk at night flashing mink stoles, diamonds, tuxes and studded canes. Atlantic City dubbed itself, "The World's Playground." All the stuff of dreams as he returned to some flop house where he slept for ten bucks a week, sharing occasional space with Polish immigrants working the summer trade, and the ever present army of cats.

He departed the inner city still in his teens, and pushed blindly into the unknown never to return, sensing to be static and do nothing would be terminal, as in fact it proved to be for many of his mates. In the decades following, he pursued new awarenesses, swam exotic currents, trekked remote tropical forests, became a soldier, ambled southwest deserts at night, slept through thunderstorms alongside petrified forests, trekked the Rockies, mastered the martial arts, jogged with blacktail deer in hills surrounding Monterey, explored Zen, motorcycled the California coast, scaled Pfeiffer Rock, freelanced, traversed the Cascades, slept beneath ancient redwoods in remote Los Padres, joined the corporate jungle, raised a family, helped birth a medical corporation, then hung up a shingle and lived on wits and ingenuity until the muse of the 60's again tapped his shoulder, ordering, "Time to shift gears, Billy."

His journey to self actualize is chronicled at www.ironcrane.com. His commitment to roots music and preserving threads of tradition can be found at www.bluemuse.org.

Made in the USA
Monee, IL
04 August 2021

74982552R00163